SHE TURNED TO THE APPROACHING ZOMBIES AND WHISTLED AT THEM AGAIN.

"Hi, boys, new in town?" she called out. "My name's Buffy and I know how to show you a real good time."

The zombie with the hole in its forehead still had two good dead eyes. It growled so deeply parts of its neck fluttered out and hit the blacktop with a sickening *plop!* Another zombie nearby scooped up the debris and stuffed it into its mouth, swallowing several of its own teeth in the process. Even though all the zombies weren't out of the tunnel yet, their leaders—that is, the ones who happened to be at the front or close to it—advanced toward Buffy.

Buffy backed up and slammed against a van. Zombies approached to the front of her. To the right of her. To the left. She looked down to see a blackened hand reaching out from beneath the van, groping for her. She ground her heel on the hand with all the might she could muster, turned, jumped, grabbed the luggage rack and swung onto the top of the van.

A zombie was already crawling up to greet her. She kicked it. The head lifted completely off the torso with a *rip* that echoed throughout the underground lot. She turned and kicked another zombie in the chest. . . .

Buffy, the Vampire Slayer™ books

#1 The Harvest
#2 Halloween Rain
#3 Coyote Moon
#4 Night of the Living Rerun

Also available
Buffy, the Vampire Slayer (movie tie-in)
 A novelization by Richie Tankersley Cusick
 Based on the screenplay by Joss Whedon

Available from ARCHWAY Paperbacks

BUFFY THE VAMPIRE SLAYER™

NIGHT OF THE LIVING RERUN

Arthur Byron Cover
Based on the hit TV series created by Joss Whedon

AN ARCHWAY PAPERBACK
Published by POCKET BOOKS
New York London Toronto Sydney Tokyo Singapore

AN ARCHWAY PAPERBACK *Original*

An Archway Paperback published by
POCKET BOOKS, a division of Simon & Schuster Inc.
1230 Avenue of the Americas, New York, NY 10020

™ and copyright © 1998 by Twentieth Century Fox Film Corporation. All rights reserved.

ISBN: 0-671-01715-2

First Archway Paperback printing March 1998

10 9 8 7 6 5 4 3 2 1

AN ARCHWAY PAPERBACK and colophon are registered trademarks of Simon & Schuster Inc.

Printed in the U.S.A.

IL 7+

Dedicated with love to my wife, Lydia.

With much thanks to David and Bobbi, Lisa and Liz, that Whedon guy, and the cast and crew of *Buffy*, especially Ken Estes for doing that video playback thing.

I'd also like to take this opportunity to say hello to my mom, my stepfather, my mother-in-law, my brothers, their wives, my nieces, my cousins, their spouses, their children, my aunts, my uncles, and everybody else associated with family values.

NIGHT OF THE LIVING RERUN

CHAPTER 1

*N*othing ever changed in the Master's lair. Nothing of importance anyway.

Oh, a few minions and undead assistants always came and went, but they fit into the nothing-of-importance category.

The Master had lived in these dreary, monotonous tunnels for nearly thirty years. By now he was deep in the process of going stark raving mad, simply from the razor-sharp dullness of virtually everything.

The Master felt he was living beneath his station. He felt like a giant, gilded cockroach, scurrying up and down the tunnels in perpetual search of an exit which did not exist.

That was on the good days. . . .

Lately the Master had become less prone to shout. For this his lowly, sniveling minions were infinitely grateful—the echoes made their ears bleed. The Master rarely shouted when a plan was going well. And recently he had bragged often about devising his most subtle, devious plan ever.

Keep in mind, the minions never saw the Master actually working on a plan. He never did *anything.*

The minions clung to the faint, doubtlessly futile hope that the Master's current plan, whatever it was, would succeed beyond his wildest expectations.

Then, the Master would be gone. Out of here. Splitsville from the Lair. At long last striding the surface of the Earth like a primordial god from the lower depths. Badder than Mars, more twisted than Hades.

On Earth the scene would be chaos, as the population found itself as close to the lower depths of the spiritual underworld as one could get without actually being there,

Thus preoccupied with a personal reign of terror of mythological proportions, the Master would have little time to devote to the insignificant minions minding his former prison.

So that down here, in the place where nothing ever happened, the unworthy minions could walk off the stage of history forever, and never have to do anything again.

Looking back, Buffy realized the entire adventure had begun long before she'd ever realized it.

When had it started? When the Master had begun his manipulations? Had it begun with the idea of the exhibition? Or when Mom had moved to Sunnydale?

Maybe it had begun with creation of the Moonman. Or perhaps with Prince Ashton Eisenberg's Prophecy of the Dual Duels. Maybe the Salem witch trials were the true beginning. It was odd to think that certain events of 1692 could have such a direct bearing on events in 1996. If stranger things had happened, Buffy did not want to know what they were.

For Buffy personally, it had begun with the dreams. At first they consisted only of a few images that recurred now and then. They had been going on for a few weeks when one afternoon in the library, Giles, from out of the blue, suggested Buffy write down her dreams first thing every morning. "Before you even get out of bed!" he insisted.

"*Why?*" Buffy asked, thinking of those images. "And why now?"

Giles shrugged. "Other Slayers have kept dream journals. It might help you get in touch with your inner warrior. " He handed her a notebook. "This should do quite nicely."

"For me? Giles, you shouldn't have."

"You're welcome, Buffy."

"Maybe I don't want to get in touch with my inner warrior. I can't be the Slayer *all* the time. Sometimes, I just want to go to sleep and forget all about this last-stand-against-evil nonsense." She stopped when she saw her friends' faces. "Forget it. Bad idea. Never mind."

"I think she's trying to say she wants a life," Willow said, typing in a series of commands without looking up from her computer screen.

"A life? Whatever do you mean?" asked Giles, taken aback at the enormity of the concept.

"Yeah, Buffy, whaddya mean?" Xander teased. "We have times, don't we?"

"Buffy, is this some kind of career thing?" Willow asked.

"A motivational problem?" Giles asked, raising one eyebrow.

Xander perked up. "A good action movie will make you forget your troubles. There's a new Jackie Chan–Jim Carrey team-up. We can go together. Tonight."

"No thanks," said Buffy, taking the notebook, "I was just under the delusion that if I kept a few private thoughts to myself, I'd have an actual private life some day. Guess I should have known better."

"You are the Slayer for this generation," said Giles, in all seriousness. "A private life is out of the question. And as the current Watcher, I should know."

"Giles, you need to get out more." Buffy said. Then she looked at the cover photo on the notebook. "Who's gramps?"

"That's Sigmund Freud," said Giles in his best you-should-already-know-this-too tone. "I thought his example as a pioneer in the exploration of the human mind might be inspirational."

"Oh yeah. He had a thing about cigars, didn't he?" Buffy handed the notebook back to Giles. "That's okay. I think I can find my own inspiration."

"As you wish," said Giles coolly.

When Buffy got home, she found her Mom unpacking a box. "New shipment?" she asked.

"Look at these! They'll fit in perfectly with the new show." Buffy's Mom held up a notebook. The photo on the front was of a sculpture of a man composed of squares and rectangles. "This is the great sculptor V.V. Vivaldi's masterpiece, 'The Moonman.'"

"Cool!" said Buffy admiring it. "I just so happen to need a new notebook."

"Then it's yours. But tell people they can see the original at the gallery."

Before she went to sleep, Buffy dutifully put the notebook and a pen on the nightstand beside her bed. She was out like a light the moment she'd put head to pillow. Her sleep was deep, deeper and colder than any she'd previously known.

When she awoke, she discovered she'd already written down her dream.

The images themselves creeped her out. There was a pulpit lying in a heap, as if smashed by a giant club. Maggots swirled around the feet of a guru whose face had been seriously rearranged.

Graves burst open with blasts of lightning, young women danced in the moonlight, and people or things passed by on the wind, only to go nuts and attack her.

Okay, so they weren't exactly the sort of dreams she'd thought she'd be having, but they were interesting, and they sort of made sense if you happened to be a Slayer.

But one image had struck her as being out of place—not really the sort of thing she'd associate with being Buffy Summers, a Slayer for the nineties—but there it was: the moon, with a huge meteor heading directly for it!

Every morning she wrote down her dreams from the night before. After about a month she reread what she'd written to see if anything struck her as noteworthy.

She was surprised to find that while some of the images were indeed random—as you'd expect in a dream—others had an internal chronological order.

The story in the dreams began through the image-distorted eyes of a little girl learning how to sew with her hands and how to cook using a huge fireplace in the kitchen. Soon she learned how to gather chestnuts and berries from the woods, and how to grind wheat for bread. When she grew older, she took to preparing the meat. Evidently she'd taken rather well to that chore, because there were a lot of images from the girl's point of view, like plucking geese and chickens and cleaning fish.

Eventually the girl reached adolescence. While the other young women were being courted by the eligible young men of whatever village this happened to be, Buffy dreamed of taking over the household hunting chores. She sensed a tragedy had happened to the head of the household that had necessitated this, but she couldn't be sure.

Her dreamself could use an ax and a knife, and a flintlock rifle whose powder had to be lit with a match before she could fire it. She was a good shot, and Buffy dreamed of bringing down turkeys at a hundred and fifty yards as well as geese and duck on the wing. She was also adept with the bow and arrow, and used them not only for hunting but for fishing as well.

There were images of people interspersed with all this sewing, cooking and hunting. Buffy had no idea who they might be, though it was reasonable to assume they were friends and family.

Around the time the girl was fifteen, the nature of the images began to change. Violently. Indians killed most of the friends and family she'd glimpsed in previous dreams, and those images were interspersed with images of herself killing Indians in return. And, as time passed in the dream, of killing all sorts of abominations. Vampires. Zombies. Demons disguised as Quakers, Indians, or British aristocrats. Stuff that struck Buffy as being rather usual. Only the time period was different.

* * *

One night, without warning, the dream became a single coherent narrative. It began with Buffy's dreamself in the middle of the square in a strange village on a starry night. Patches of ice-hard snow were on the ground. The clean, neat square was illuminated by a series of oil lamps. At one end stood a huge wooden church, its position in relation to the shops and offices designating it as the most important place in the community.

In the center of the square was a gallows. A group of angry men in plain black suits pushed a young man wearing a cleric's collar toward the steps leading up to the hangman's noose. A few of the men carried old-fashioned flintlock rifles, the kind where the powder and bullet were loaded separately. Occasionally, when the young man wasn't moving fast enough, they prodded him with the rifle barrels.

Buffy looked down. Her dreamself sat astride a horse; across the saddle laid her flintlock, loaded and ready for bear. A muscle twitched in her wrist. She calculated how fast she could reload, and how many men she might shoot if they rushed her.

She sighed; such an approach was not worthy of the righteous. She fired her flintlock. Into the air.

Some of the men gasped, others denounced her or shook their fists, but none made a move toward her. Her hands and powderbag were a blur as she reloaded faster than any had ever imagined possible.

She pointed the weapon directly at the man at

the forefront. "Forgive me, gentlemen, I usually refrain from interfering with matters of justice—"

The man was large and fat, but clearly possessed great confidence and personal power. He looked up at her defiantly. Behind his brave smile, however, lay profound fear, though whether it was directed at Buffy's dreamself or at the situation in general was a little hard to tell. "Samantha Kane. I might have known. You are tardy once again."

"I was delayed."

"By the presence of evil, I presume?"

Samantha Kane shrugged. "What is evil in your eyes, sir, is not necessarily evil in mine."

She lowered her flintlock and got off her horse. The crowd of men whispered furtively among themselves. Samantha Kane did not care. She knew they thought her unusual. Women in this day and age did not ride horseback, they did not travel alone, they were not marksmen, and they never, *never* were feared by common rabble. Such women would have been accused of witchcraft, found guilty regardless of the mitigating circumstances and hanged.

Yet no one dared accuse Samantha Kane of witchcraft. Her reputation precluded that. "It is good to see you, Judge Danforth, though I wish the circumstances were more pleasant."

"Circumstances are never pleasant in these perilous times, Goodwoman Kane. You are well?" He looked at her kindly, the fear in his eyes replaced by a great weariness.

"I am well. And you, my friend?" Samantha regarded this Judge Danforth as an ally, though she still harbored suspicions about him.

"Well enough to carry out my sad duties. This poor wretch has just been pronounced guilty of practicing the rites of a warlock and of consorting with a witch. The sentence is to be carried out immediately."

"Immediately?"

Danforth shrugged and frowned. "Normally those found guilty of consorting with the devil are given twenty-fours to contemplate the error of their ways and ask for forgiveness, in the hope that their soul may be redeemed. But this wretch"—the judge sneered—"was a protégé of mine. I had high hopes that he would one day become a righteous leader of the community and would save many souls. It saddens me greatly to see how far he has fallen."

Samantha looked the "wretch" in the eye. They were golden, sensitive eyes, and she found herself liking them.

"Your name, sir," Samantha demanded.

He regarded her coldly. "I am the Right Reverend John Goodman. And you are Samantha Kane, the witch-hunter."

"Among other things." She noted his clothing was filthy as a result of his imprisonment, but he still wore the white collar of the clergy despite his fallen status. His face was bruised and his long red hair was matted. She supposed he was holding up pretty well for a man who was about to be hanged.

"You people," Samantha said to the crowd, and especially to a man pouring whale oil over the wood, "just wait."

"Why?" sneered one, who obviously thought her no different than the rest of the witches.

Samantha grabbed him by the frills of his waistcoat, pulled his face close to hers and growled softly, "Because it is not a good night to die." She released him, then looked around. "Your 'warlock' can die tomorrow night just as easily."

Judge Danforth took her by the arm and drew her gently away from Goodman and the crowd. "Are you defending this man?" he asked patiently. "This *devil worshipper?*"

"I know I missed Goodman's accusation and trial because I was away dispatching abominations in New York," said Samantha, flashing on an image of the natives rising from their burial grounds to attack a town meeting, "but I have reason to suspect you and the others have been duped. I would know more."

Shocked, Danforth said, "First, Goodman denounced a woman as a witch. Second, after we debated the evidence and came to our decision to try the woman, he was nowhere to be found. He only reappeared after she'd been found guilty and was scheduled to be punished. Third, soon after he visited her in the witch dungeon, she made good her escape. The witch is still at large. What more evidence is needed to conclude he is in league with the devil?"

"How righteous is the tribunal who sanctions the execution of an innocent man?" Samantha shot back. "I would know more!"

"For instance?" Danforth asked.

"Was this witch accused on his word alone? Or are there others who believe this woman in league with the devil?"

Danforth's mouth curled up. He nodded to a man Samantha recognized as Sheriff Corwin, who in turn nodded to the man Samantha had pushed around. "Bring out the girls," said Sheriff Corwin, "bring them out immediately and show her the devil is not in New York, nor Williamsburg, nor any other place people believe him to be. It is 1692, and the devil is here in Salem."

Salem in 1692! Buffy almost jolted awake. This past Slayer had operated smack in the midst of the witch hunts in Salem, Massachusetts. It was one of the most notorious incidents in early American colonial history. Buffy had learned a lot about it from renting horror films.

The man Samantha had pushed around glared at her. "This is your fault, woman. You deny me justice."

"If what you want is just, it will not be denied," Samantha replied. "Now please, sir, do as you have been asked."

"This is Joseph Putnam," said Judge Danforth.

"His daughter Heather is one of the girls he must fetch to satisfy your curiosity. Go, man, and let us do what must be done."

He went. Samantha barely noticed. "It is not mere curiosity that causes me to question your wisdom."

"Though that is certainly true in part."

"Yes."

Samantha and the men waited in silence. Fireflies flew everywhere, reflecting in the eyes of the angry crowd. Goodman stood calmly, unmoving, looking at her. A breeze ruffled his long hair. Samantha was impressed by his bravery. She felt that under different circumstances, they might have been friends.

She saw no reason why she should not fight for his survival. After all, was she not charged with protecting the innocent as well as eradicating abominations?

"He is the one!" cried out a young girl hysterically. "He is the one responsible for my delirium!" The material and workmanship of the girl's dress marked her as a member of a wealthy merchant family, yet the sleeves were tattered and many stitches were torn. The girl's eyes were wild, and fresh red scratches marred her ivory complexion.

Samantha recognized her as Heather Putnam. She noted the tips of Heather's fingers were bloody; the girl had injured herself, an indication of contamination by the devil himself if ever there was one.

Back in the twentieth century, Buffy ascribed her condition to hysteria, pure and simple.

Heather and two others approximately the same age and in the same general condition were bound at the waist by a single rope. Putnam and four other men were required to hold the rope in order to drag them in the desired direction. Having brought them this far, the men were now obliged to hold the girls in their place to prevent them from lunging at Reverend Goodman and, presumably, scratching out his eyes.

Putnam's mind was not on his job. He stared mournfully at his daughter and occasionally wiped a tear from his eye.

Danforth shook his head in pity at the girls. Goodman, on the other hand, muttered a prayer for them. The men in the crowd regarded them with horror.

"He is responsible! He is the one!" the girls said. "He is responsible!"

"I thought you said the slave woman was responsible for your condition," Danforth protested.

The girls got very quiet. Heather frowned, deep in thought. The other two pointedly looked at her, if silently asking for direction. Heather nodded. Then, almost in unison, they proclaimed, "The slave is responsible too! Tituba is the one! Tituba is the one!"

"Do you see?" Danforth calmly asked Samantha. "They are all quite mad. And very easily confused. Each and every one. Obviously the work of the devil."

Samantha's sharp retort formed in Buffy's mind, but the dreamworld of the past was suddenly obliterated in a flash of red light, and Buffy realized, with a groan, that she had fallen out of bed.

"Buffy!" shouted her mother from down the hall. "Are you all right?"

CHAPTER 2

Buffy began her morning ritual of tai chi exercises at the first sign of dawn. She tried not to think about her dream. What had seemed so supremely exciting now seemed vaguely unnatural. Obviously the best thing to do would be to relax, so she could face the day with a clear head.

That decided, Buffy checked out her appearance in the mirror on her dresser. And practically fainted: There was a bruise the size of Kansas on her forehead.

Later, at breakfast, Mom was preoccupied with advertising the V.V. Vivaldi exhibition at the gallery (which she was sure would bring in a lot of business), but she did find time to make it clear— for the umpteenth time—that Buffy's pretty skin wasn't going to keep its pure, youthful quality too long if she kept banging it up all the time.

Buffy shrugged, absently tossing her butter knife into the open dishwasher.

The dishwasher happened to be across the kitchen. The butterknife had sailed through the **air** end-over-end and landed handle up.

It was followed in quick succession by the rest of Buffy's silverware. Each piece landed perfectly in the rack. Buffy paused, twirling her steak knife in one hand like it was a baton.

Mom sat there silent and slack-jawed. "Buffy—?"

Buffy remembered she had an audience. "It's, ah, something we've been learning in Home Ec." She threw the steak knife.

And missed. Completely.

It landed in the sink. Buffy picked up her glass and moved toward the dishwasher.

"Ah, wait a minute there!" interrupted Mom. "Why not do the rest the old-fashioned way."

"Oh, we never throw the dinnerware."

Her mother looked relieved.

"Not until next semester."

Buffy walked to school under a cloud. She'd been so distracted by the dream that she'd gotten sloppy and let her mother see something that reminded her of when Buffy had burned down the school gym—a big *no-no* in the mother's manual. Mom had said a thousand times that if she caught Buffy doing anything that smacked of that kind of trouble again, she would ground her indefinitely.

Buffy believed her. She didn't want to have to explain to Giles that she couldn't save the world from a wave of enraged soul-eaters because she was chained to her bedpost.

The only silver lining in her cloud was the knowledge that soon she could confide to Willow about the dream. She wanted to tell Willow first because Giles would just try to explain it all away with facts and theories, and something about the experience was simply too fantastic for that. Buffy didn't want to spoil it, yet.

The only problem, as it turned out, was Xander, who knew their schedules better than they did and hence did not miss an opportunity when it came to finding one of them. Today he simply would not go away when Buffy and Willow made it clear his presence wasn't welcome at the moment.

Consequently, Buffy was probably harsher than necessary when she finally told him to get lost.

"Why?" Xander asked. "We always study in the library together."

Giles cleared his throat but refrained from looking up from the massive, dusty tome he'd been studying since they'd come in.

"You too—out!" Buffy pleaded. "Willow and I need to be alone."

"We do?" said Willow.

"Yeah. You know, girl stuff: hair, nails . . ."

"Clothes, boys." Willow quickly added.

Giles closed the book and said with mock resignation, "Come along, Xander, I guess even a Vampire Slayer needs a private moment once in a while. Besides, this will give us a chance to discuss certain astrological portents we need researched."

"Right now?"

"Why dally where we're not wanted?"

"I'll want a complete report later!" said Xander over his shoulder, as Giles led him away.

"He must think you want to confide in me about your personal life," Willow whispered, barely containing her excitement. "Is it about boys? You do want to talk about boys, don't you?" She was visibly crestfallen when Buffy, who suddenly had second thoughts, countered with:

"Well, no. I need to talk about history."

"You're kidding."

"No. I've got some questions about colonial times. I'm afraid I haven't always been paying attention in class."

"So what else is new? You've been daydreaming about boys, right?"

"No, I've been taking catnaps because I've been up all hours of the night keeping the world safe from the scum of the nether-regions."

"Oh, now I understand why you're so interested in history all of a sudden," said Willow, her sigh indicating her reluctant acceptance. "We are, after all, having a big test this afternoon."

All the blood drained from Buffy's face. "This afternoon? Today? Or this afternoon, tomorrow?"

Willow checked her watch. "Today. In about twenty minutes, to be precise."

"What kind of test is it?"

"Probably multiple choice, or in your case, multiple guess. That way it'll be easy for Mrs. Honneger to grade. She likes doing homework about as much as we do."

"So, why don't you ask me a few questions?" said Buffy, trying to relax. Tension always worked against her when she was trying to recall facts for a test, though strangely, it always seemed to help when the situation called for arcane vampire lore or sophisticated combat improvisation.

"Okay, what year was Plymouth Colony founded?"

"1620!"

"Who founded it?"

"The Puritans, who were fleeing religious persecution in England."

"And what did they want ?" Willow asked, her eyes narrowing.

"A place where they could enjoy religious freedom. But that's where they sorta screwed up. 'Cause the only religion they allowed was their own. Dissenters were punished—banished! Did you know that?"

"I knew that. What was name of their colony?"

"The Massachusetts Bay Colony."

"What kind of government did they practice?"

"A theocracy, meaning government by interpretation of the religious scriptures. Preachers had quite a bit of influence, since officeholders always had to look to them for approval."

Willow pursed her lips. "Buffy, you *have* been studying, haven't you? On the sly, right?"

"Uh, right."

"What can you tell me about the witch trials of 1692?"

"Not too much," said Buffy. "A group of girls about our age became afflicted with convulsive fits, short-term hearing, seeing, and memory loss, and strange bruises and marks on the skin! The local doctors didn't know what to call it, so their diagnosis was witchcraft! By the time the preachers, judges and sheriffs got involved, there was a full-scale panic. At that time, anything that couldn't be explained was blamed on the supernatural!"

"Mrs. Honneger never told us that!"

"Did you know that one of the first people to be accused was a slave named Tituba, who on dark and stormy nights fed the girls tales of possession and the walking dead? Tituba survived, actually, because she repented. Mrs. Honneger thinks the girls were faking their symptoms, but the problem could have been entirely medical or psychological in origin! Or maybe they just wanted the attention!"

Buffy became pensive. "You know, if you put together the changing social and political structure of the colony with the people's view of a world where the devil and his demons were actively conspiring against them—then the Salem Witch Trials were almost inevitable. Besides, hysteria over witches had been going on in Europe for a couple of centuries, and there they were burned at the stake, rather than merely hanged."

"I wouldn't worry too much about this test if I were you," Willow said.

Just then Giles stalked back in, followed by Xander, who was barely keeping his mirth to himself. Giles wore a stern expression on his face.

"I hope you ladies are through with your little talk," Giles said, "because I suspect a situation is brewing right under our very noses."

Buffy sighed. "Another emergency? No prob. I can probably fit it in between history and math."

Xander giggled.

Giles looked at him sternly. "This isn't funny. The human race could be doomed to extinction."

"I'm sorry," said Xander, in tones that indicated he really wasn't, "but you're getting all worked up about a prophecy made two hundred years ago by some guy even you admit was insane."

"He doesn't sound too reliable," said Willow, as Buffy gestured at Xander to stop snickering. Which Xander did, but with difficulty.

Giles cleared his throat, then plunged right ahead. "I have been studying *The Eibon*. It is the most notorious book of prophecies ever written, with the possible exception of two lost books referred to in that great cycle of East Indian mythology, *The Mahabharata*. Unlike those two lost books, however, *The Eibon* is still with us. An early copy is almost always in the possession of the Watcher, passed down from the previous occupant of that post.

"You've heard, of course, of Nostradamus, Cayce, Criswell—the great seers of modern Western thought who saw far into the future and then wrote it down, in the hope their wisdom would be handed down to subsequent generations. Their major predictions tend to be deliberately vague, so it's possible to draw many different meanings from them. Some people, for instance, believe Nostradamus predicted the advent of the airplane and tank as weapons during World War I, while others believe the same verse refers to the approach of the tropical weather phenomenon known as *el niño*. Personally, I think they're both wrong, but nobody's been asking me my opinion lately."

"Is that such a surprise?" asked Xander, unable to resist the line. He was mildly frustrated when everyone pointedly ignored him.

"Greatest of all was the mad Austrian heretic Prince Ashton Eisenberg V, who lived from 1692 till 1776. Toward the end of his life, when he was imprisoned in the Bastille in Paris—thanks to being caught in the midst of some indiscretion—he wrote a book of prophecies unparalleled in their precision. When he writes that the snake-brother's army shall devour the parasitic brother's army in the New World, for instance, he's obviously referring to the American Civil War, nearly a century later."

"Obviously," agreed Willow.

Caught up in his lecture, Giles continued, "Prince Ashton's most famous prediction is known simply as Eisenberg's Prophecy of the Dual Duel. It's the vaguest of all his predictions. Roughly translated from its pidgin German, it says:

> There came a time when the planets and stars were in harmony
> A time when that which was before, shall be again,
> And that which was done, will be done again.
> A time when a great beast shall crawl onto the land,
> A beast beyond defeat but not beyond loss
> A beast who shall be vanquished by the pure in heart.
> Such a time shall come again.
> As surely as the stars will once again be in similiar harmony
> And at this time another beast shall rise,
> A beast different in body but same in spirit
> And like his brother of old he shall strive

*To steal the moon, to consume the sun, and to
  walk the earth.*

*To see if he might strike a dagger into the heart
  of destiny.*

"Interesting, wouldn't you say?" Giles eagerly
awaited their response.

"Actually, the word I was thinking of was far-
fetched," said Xander.

"I think I'm leaning toward Xander's point of
view on this one," said Buffy. "Tell me again how
accurate this guy was—"

"—on matters other than this great beast thing,"
Willow suggested.

Giles smiled, weakly. "There are some who
believe Prince Ashton Eisenberg predicted night
baseball."

"Before or after the invention of satellite television?" Xander asked, smartly.

"Before."

"Wow," said Xander breathlessly. "He *was*
good."

"So when did the first great beast try to walk the
earth?" asked Willow.

"The beast in question was an abomination
called the Despised One. The Despised One tried
to rise from the nether-regions sometime around
the year of Prince Ashton's birth—"

"1692!" exclaimed Buffy.

"And it happened somewhere in the New World.
Now, I grant you old Ashton was certifiable, but he

is a towering figure in occult studies because so many of his prophecies have come true. He claimed the ghost of the Despised One communicated with him occasionally and discussed strategies to shift the traditional balance between good and evil. Ashton approached the occult rather scientifically, so when a routine examination verified the beast's information, he realized the strategy could be repeated, but only at particular times, when rather specific conditions are met.

"I don't know about most of the conditions, but the stars are getting right. And that means we could be in the midst of it and not even know it yet."

"1692," said Xander soberly. "That's the year of the Salem witch trials. Which happens to be one of the subjects we're being tested on in history class today."

The bell rang, indicating study period was over.

"A test which is right about now," said Willow.

The moment Buffy laid down her pen in history class, she knew she'd aced the test. Answers had come to her so easily she'd had to force herself to slow down, just in case Mrs. Honneger had thrown a few trick questions into the mix.

After midnight that evening, she snuck out of the house to foil an insane circus clown's plot to infest the Sunnydale rat population with piranha DNA. The clown, it seemed, held a grudge against the town after some environmental mishap he had suffered during his youth.

Buffy was successful—but not until the clown had been devoured by his own creations. Unfortunately, while eluding the horde of mutant rodents by crawling through a flooded basement, Buffy came down with a serious cold.

By the time the rats lay dead in a giant heap before a statue of the blindfolded lady justice, Buffy could barely breathe, and she was sweating like she'd done an intense workout on a hundred-degree day.

Immediately after sneaking back into the house, she took a cold shower to try to get her temperature to drop. Once again she was out the moment her head struck the pillow. Her hair was still wrapped in a towel and her body didn't seem cooler by even one degree.

Her mind fell through a sea of holes. It landed on an infinity of nothingness.

And she was back. Back as Samantha Kane, intrepid witch-hunter in 1692 Massachusetts; but the Salem gallows, the angry men and Heather Putnam and her co-conspirators were nowhere around.

Samantha was alone, on horseback, in the cross-roads of two trails in a daylit wood. She had followed the escaped Sarah Dinsdale's footsteps to this point, but now they had suddenly disappeared.

No matter, Buffy heard Samantha thinking, *she'll reveal herself another way. They always do.*

Samantha's mount was jittery. Her own horse was spent, so she'd borrowed this mount from Judge Danforth, but it wasn't used to being ridden as hard as Samantha needed it to.

The rays of the setting sun reflected off something down the eastern fork. Samantha jerked the reins to get the horse's attention, then rode it roughly to the place where she'd seen the glint.

Buffy mumbled in her sleep, "The way you're treating that mare, it's a wonder she doesn't throw you in a briar patch."

Samantha dismounted and lifted a bright orange piece of cloth shaped like the letter "W" from where it was caught on top of a bramble bush. It was the mark of a witch—customarily sewn onto the clothing of a devil's consort once sentence was passed.

One thing was obvious: Sarah Dinsdale had taken the eastern fork.

Samantha spurred her horse onward. Night fell quickly this time of year, and the slayer knew she must find Sarah soon, or she would lose her under cover of darkness.

But by late dusk Samantha realized the witch had left no further evidence of her passing this way, indeed, if she had taken this direction in the first place.

Samantha brought her horse to a halt and fumed.

Flummoxed by a witch! She felt very stupid, which made her very, very angry.

Suddenly the walls of the dream shifted a few hours into the night. The seventeenth-century Slayer sat by a campfire. She was alone, without a captor to keep her company; even the corpse of a witch would have been an improvement, because then Samantha would have had her satisfaction to keep her warm.

The forest was quiet, devoid of insect noises and animal calls, and it was still—no breeze rustled the leaves, no animal wandered about. Not even the owls hooted in the trees.

Samantha knew this silence was unnatural. The forest was a live, vibrant place. It was this quiet only when the presence of some malevolent force made it so.

Samantha yawned. She had been traveling nonstop for the past three weeks and had expected to rest once in Salem. She needed time to refresh herself, and to think. It didn't appear she'd have it anytime soon.

She tore off a piece of dried meat with her teeth, sat on a log and watched the fire. Samantha didn't regret being the Slayer of this time—in fact, she rather enjoyed ridding the earth of unclean abominations—but she disliked the lonely nights.

She thought of roads she might have taken, opportunities seemingly offered up by God's will millions of years ago. In truth, only eight years had passed since Samantha had first embarked on the quest, but each year seemed like a lifetime.

Suddenly—what? A sound of some sort, but it ceased almost the moment it began.

It had happened there, in the brush.

Samantha picked up her flintlock—she'd refilled the powder just this morning—and with her other hand took a torch from the fire.

Her every sound was accentuated, from the crunching of pebbles underfoot to the soft rustle of a branch she shifted to get a better look at the place from which the sound had come. None of those noises, however, could match the pounding, pounding, pounding of her heart. She was convinced the thunder in her chest and temples could be heard all the way to New York.

A cluster of leaves and twigs near the ground moved.

The thunder stopped; Samantha's heart felt like it had collapsed. But a bittersweet taste in her mouth forestalled the fear. It was the taste she always got when she knew she was in the presence of an abomination. Every chance she had to rid the Earth of one of those infernal things made her thrilled to be alive. And every thrill erased a thousand regrets.

She moved in, wishing for a third arm so that she might hold forth her rapier as well.

She shook the torch and yelled. Not the most cautious move, but certain impulses toward danger were among her more self-destructive traits.

The move worked. Fortunately or not—mostly not, from Buffy's perspective. Because *it* darted out! And it was charging full out like a giant spider, weaving from side to side with every step, yet never wavering from its basic direction: straight toward Samantha Kane!

It leapt, grabbing Samantha's throat with gray, decomposing fingers that were amazingly strong. They squeezed Samantha's neck. *Hard.*

Samantha dropped her torch and her pistol and grabbed *it* by the stump at the end of its hand. Actually, that's all it was—a disembodied hand, but it was one that could move of its own accord, with a will of its own. Samantha couldn't pry the fingers loose. Her face and lungs felt like they were about to explode.

She suddenly remembered her knife. She began butchering the hand. Tearing off the skin was easy: the hand was about the size of a rabbit, and Samantha had skinned plenty of those.

She whittled away at the muscles, yet the bones of the fingers squeezed just as hard on their own. They had no need of muscles—exactly the sort of thing Samantha had come to expect from such sorcerous vileness.

One by one, she cut the finger bones from the hand. Lacking even a palm, the fingers still tried to hang onto her throat. Samantha had to break them off with her own hands.

She seethed with anger and shivered in disgust. With the simplest of lures, the witch had drawn

Samantha into a trap. This really gnawed at Samantha's pride—she was the best hunter and tracker in the northern colonies who didn't wear war paint and worship like a heathen, and she'd been tricked like a novice.

Samantha noticed her mount was nervous and was trying to pull its reins free.

She picked up another torch from the fire and somewhat impulsively, but with a growing sense of horror, peered deeper into the bush.

Other body parts approached: Another hand walked on fingers. One full arm and the two halves of another rolled toward her. At least the head was still attached—though to a legless torso. That meant the head and torso had to pull themselves forward with the use of the neck, teeth and chin, a process that had wreaked havoc with the corpse's freshly decaying flesh.

The eyes looked toward Samantha. The head tilted sideways so it could speak more easily. "Samantha," the broken mouth said. "I've come for you. Wait for me. . . ."

Now Samantha knew what had happened. Sarah had used her witchcraft after coming upon, and perhaps butchering, this pitiful wretch. Then she had placed a spell on the pieces to find and kill Samantha.

Samantha took aim at the center of head with her flintlock. She fired once, and the disembodied head's skull and brain exploded in all directions.

That didn't stop the other body parts, though.

They were still coming for her, as quick as they were able.

Obviously the time had come to leave. Samantha kicked out the fire, got on her horse and lit out with all possible speed, using only the moonlight to guide her.

CHAPTER 3

*T*he gathering was a spontaneous event to which everyone had been invited. It was being held in a giant cavern on the outskirts of the Lair, lit by fires whose embers burned farther below than anyone wanted to know.

Any normal person would have found the heat outrageous, yet those here thought it rather comfortable. The crowd focused their attention on the stage, which featured a podium, a microphone and a picture of the Master that took up the entire rear curtain.

Equally spontaneous was the deafening roar the crowd made at the behest of a few minions when the Master walked onto the stage. Bathed in a spotlight, the Master took a few bows, waved at a few demons he had a professional relationship with and then basked in the general adulation.

The entire affair was climaxed by the unexpected appearance of the biggest, baddest fallen angel in the hierarchy of evil—Old Scratch himself! He presented to the stunned, humble Master a plaque inscribed To the Master of Evil, Exceptin' Old Scratch Himself.

"Sire! Does this mean you're setting me free?"

"Not a chance, skull-face," Old Scratch said, drawing a big laugh from the crowd. "Now go away, boy, you bother me!"

The crowd roared, seeing the Master wallowing in his own hotheaded despair.

The Master reached out for the hooves at the end of Old Scratch's legs. "Don't do it! I beg you! Just tell me what you want to do to me and I'll inflict the same unspeakable punishment on somebody else! Please!"

Old Scratch did not respond. He did not even use that hideous gurgle of boiling hot blood reserved for any cowering servant who had committed the most serious transgression. In fact, come to think of it, there weren't even those great, rock-hard hooves about. The Master could not find them to grab.

The Master took a chance and looked up. Old Scratch was nowhere to be seen. The crowd, the lights and the stage were gone. The Master was back in his underground prison, wallowing on one of the tunnel floors.

He had been asleep. Dreaming. A nightmare.

The Master chuckled as he stood up. The cheap irony did not escape him: He too had been using dreams to serve his own ends. He thought it excellent that his own subconscious had reminded him what powerful, unpredictable forces dreams could be.

The others, however, wouldn't so lucky. They didn't have his unique insight into the unnatural order of things. And because they lacked this knowledge, the Slayer, her Watcher and her chattering lackeys would be dust, and he would rule his rightful realm once more.

The Master laughed until the echoes rang up and down the tunnels like a scream from an infinite abyss. Even his minions, who had thought they were immune to most effects of complete, abject fear, quivered in their three-toed boots.

Xander and Willow caught up with Buffy on her way to school. Childhood friends, their conversation often revolved around matters Buffy couldn't possibly relate to.

Today, their preoccupation with their kindergarten days left her free to brood over her dreams. Given all that Giles had said, the dreams had to be regarded with suspicion.

What she'd revealed to Willow about her knowledge of the period was only the beginning. Buffy found she knew things about the people of Salem and North Salem that couldn't have been learned from any history book.

Including the inner joy that had surged through Samantha Kane when she'd slain her first vampire.

They were only a few blocks away from the Sunnydale High rear entrance when Buffy became vaguely aware of someone trying to get their attention.

He was a late-middle-aged man in a baggy old suit, with a bowtie and a battered old hat. He carried a large, old-fashioned flash camera.

"You're that newspaper reporter I saw on TV last week," said Xander before the man could open his mouth, "the one who believes mad cow disease was caused by the ghosts of buffalo who'd been forced to cross the Atlantic for Buffalo Bill's traveling Wild West Show in the 1890s!"

"No, no, it's more complicated than that," the man replied defensively. "My words were taken out of context."

"This gentleman shows up a lot on the Channel Three News 'Conspiracy Theory of the Week' slot," Xander explained to the girls. "I forget his name—"

"Darryl MacGovern," said the reporter.

"He also broke the story to the supermarket rags about the outbreak of three-legged frogs in Spokane, Washington," continued Xander. "And he claims the animated TV show *Teenage Mutant Two-Fisted Possums* is actually propaganda created by aliens to prepare us for what they look like when they invade the planet."

"I never said that!" protested MacGovern. "Not exactly, anyway!"

"So you work for Channel Three?" asked Willow, trying to be casual.

"No, they just use me for their conspiracy segment whenever they can't find anything else suitably outrageous. "

"So, if you only do TV part-time, who else do you work for?" Buffy asked suspiciously.

"The *Clayton Press,*" said MacGovern. "Well, to be honest, I used to work there. The publisher fired me three weeks ago. Apparently he found my frequent appearances on a show about conspiracy theories compromised my integrity as a reporter." He snorted. "As if such a thing were possible."

"It's a cruel world, but sometimes it's a fair one," said Xander.

"So what brings you to Sunnydale High?" asked Buffy innocently, though she had a bad feeling about this.

"A story!" said MacGovern enthusiastically. "One so fantastic the paper'll beg me to come back. But I'll have enough name-value recognition to start my own exposé show."

"On Channel Three?" Willow asked.

"No! On the Occult Channel!" MacGovern exclaimed. "I'll make cable after this!"

"You may smell a story," said Buffy, "but I smell a *rat!*"

MacGovern leaned into her. "Perhaps you can help me. I understand a lot of peculiar doings have been going on in Sunnydale lately."

"No kidding," said Buffy dryly. "Nobody told me!"

"Things are pretty quiet around here," said Xander. He and Willow yawned.

"I have this talent for stumbling across things that defy rational explanation. The frustrating part is, no matter what I do, no matter how careful I am, I can never get to the bottom of a story without losing all my tangible proof!"

"So why are you here?" Willow asked with a smile. She couldn't help herself; she thought this guy was funny.

"A few weeks ago, I realized I was coming out of a cloud. Something had been nagging at my natural curiosity for months, yet I'd been unable to verbalize it. I mean, it's my business to know whether or not something's any of my business. Understand what I'm talking about?"

Buffy got a sinking feeling, as if her stomach were being thrown over a ravine with the rest of her soon to follow.

"In fact, I realized I'd heard a whole lot of unsubstantiated rumors about things that were happening in Sunnydale. So after about sixteen hours pondering over the situation from the vantage point of the conspiracy theory pages on the Web, I did some research in the files of the *Clayton Press* and other major suburban newspapers in the vicinity. And you know what I found? Of course you don't. I discovered nothing."

The three teens looked at each other in confusion.

"Nothing?" Willow echoed.

"Exactly! And that's the whole point!"

"No kidding," said Willow sympathetically. "You look a little pale. Have you been taking all your mineral supplements?"

"No. Listen, no town has *nothing*. Everybody has *something*. Something to hide. Something to deny—"

"No we don't!" Xander tried.

"Yeah," Buffy echoed. "We don't have nothing. . . ." She trailed off. "Where was I?"

An awkward silence passed between the reporter and everyone else. Buffy stewed, betrayed by fate in the form of a nosy flat-footed reporter, yet she had to struggle to conceal her emotions. The tendency of most people not to believe what's right in front of them, which had enabled her to live a semblance of a normal life, was now playing tricks with her. She could only wonder how many people might be noticing, for the first time, the events that had recently occurred in Sunnydale thanks to the existence of the Hellmouth below.

"So what are you trying to tell us?" asked Willow aggressively—which was unusual in itself.

"Nothing!" MacGovern answered forcefully.

"So you're telling us you're going to hunt for nothing?" Buffy spoke slowly as if to a child.

"Exactly!" MacGovern seemed excited someone finally understood. "I'm going to find this nothing and expose it as something!"

"Uh-oh gotta split!" said Xander suddenly. He took MacGovern's hand and pumped it vigorously. "Gonna be late!"

"Can't miss homeroom!" said Willow.

"Nice meeting you," said Buffy, leading the others away. "Good luck finding nothing."

"So, Giles, still searching for portents of things to come?" Xander asked briskly as he entered the library with Buffy and Willow. They often stopped by right after school just to see if anything was going down.

The Eibon is nothing to joke about," replied Giles sternly.

"What else we know about this Prince Ashton Eisenberg besides the fact he was two tamales short of a full plate?" Willow asked.

"Reliable sources say he died as a result of spontaneous combustion," said Giles, "that is, his body burned up of its own accord, without benefit of fuel or match."

"Fascinating," said Buffy. "But we've got a problem."

"You first," said Giles, with a smile.

"Okay." Quickly she told Giles about their encounter with Darryl MacGovern.

"It's bad, isn't it?" Xander asked.

"It's worse—it's disastrous!" Giles exclaimed. "This MacGovern character is a veritable *stalkerazzi,* well-known in legitimate scholarly occult circles as a complete pest. He never rests until he gets his story or meets a total dead end, whichever comes first."

"At least we can always use Xander as a decoy until we can throw him off the scent entirely," said Willow with a sigh.

"Thanks a lot," said Xander.

"It's a good plan," said Giles, "but I bet MacGovern is just a pawn in some greater game. He may be only an insignificant red herring, sent to throw us off the real scent while the real pieces come into play."

"Maybe we should introduce him to the Master," said Xander. "Then MacGovern will start bugging *him* for an exclusive."

"We could," said Willow, "but that would be wrong."

"Giles, what did you mean by 'You first'?" asked Buffy.

"Last night I had a dream that disturbed me greatly," Giles replied.

Buffy literally bit her tongue.

"It was so vivid, so real—it was unlike any dream I had ever experienced. After all, it had a coherent narrative—at least as much as the events it portrayed allowed it to be."

"Were these actual historical events?" Buffy asked.

"As near as I can determine, yes," said Giles. "I was clearly dreaming about a past life. I have long suspected I might be the reincarnation of an earlier Watcher or two, but never in my wildest flights of fancy did I think I might be spiritually related to the legendary late-seventeenth-century Watcher Robert Erwin."

"What were you doing in the dream?" asked Willow.

"Not very much," said Giles. "I'm afraid I had succumbed to a raging fever and was delirious. Robert Erwin thought the fever had supernatural origins, which I tended to agree with."

"Oh come on!" said Xander. "The supernatural can't explain everything! Maybe he was just sick!"

"That is possible, but I remember his paranoid ravings quite clearly," said Giles. "Anyway, Erwin was under the care of an innkeeper and his wife in Boston. Of course he was worried about what the late seventeenth-century Slayer was up to."

"Who was she?" asked Buffy dryly. She thought she would like to hear what Giles knew before offering collaborating evidence.

"Her name was Samantha Kane, and she made quite a reputation for herself. She was described in letters and certain official writings as a sort of Joan of Arc type, in that she could perform with ease tasks formerly thought only the province of men."

"I like her already," said Willow slyly.

"So do I," replied Giles. "Unfortunately it seems that poor Robert Erwin was unable to assist Samantha Kane as he so clearly desired to. He died of his fever, and she disappears entirely from the historical record around 1692, during the height of the infamous Salem witch trials."

CHAPTER 4

"**S**ure we should be doing this?" Buffy asked Giles, as she deftly deflected a thrust of his *kitana*—a Japanese practice sword—with her staff. "Aren't you worried that MacGovern might be spying on us?" Shifting her weight, she swung her weapon sideways, taking Giles's feet out from under him.

He landed heavily on his back with a satisfactory thump. "Of course," he gasped. He rolled over and coughed. "But he'll probably attempt to verify his facts before trying to sell the story to his editors. After all, he needs to fill an entire show and be prepared to go on some cable news channel to defend his story."

She reached down to help him stand. "Where did you learn that move?" he asked.

"From an old movie on TV," said Buffy proudly. "I think it starred somebody—Flynn, or maybe what's-his-name—Lancaster, I forget which. Are we done?"

"No, we must complete the session." He rubbed his back and groaned. "As difficult as that might prove to be."

"Okay! But don't say I didn't warn you—I've been watching a lot of old movies lately."

"I was afraid of that." Stiffly, Giles assumed a fighting position. "This is called a wombat stance—"

"Looks more like a drunken squirrel to me," Buffy giggled.

He sliced sideways with the *kitana*. When she avoided it—easily—he grabbed her arm, twisted around and tried to throw her over his shoulder. But she was too fast. Using their momentum, she landed on her feet, pivoted around to face him and grabbed him by the collar. With one smooth movement she threw herself backwards and, with the help of her foot on his chest, she threw him across the room.

Buffy picked up her staff as she lept to her feet, ready for his next move, exactly as she would do had she been facing a genuine foe. "Can I go home now?" she asked, pleadingly.

"No," Giles groaned. He reached out for a helping hand, which pointedly did not arrive.

"What is the point of this lesson?" she asked.

"Perseverance," said Giles pulling himself to his feet. "And patience against an opponent who doesn't know when he's been beaten." He tried to jab her with the *kitana* handle.

She dodged the blow easily, grabbed his wrist, twisted the *kitana* from his hand, elbowed him against the chin just hard enough so he knew she could do it, and then she sent him flying again.

He slid across the top of the desk like a stone skipping across a lake, and then hit the floor.

Fortunately Giles wore elbow, knee and chest pads whenever he worked out with Buffy, but now he considered just buying a padded suit to cover every inch of his body. "I am convinced, Buffy, that if demons and other ghouls don't do in this particular Watcher someday, his favorite Slayer will manage to do the job for him."

"Sorry about that. I really want to go home today. By the way, what was that stance again? The wombat?" Buffy attempted to imitate the stance Giles had taken.

Giles blinked until he got her into better focus, then said, "Hold the right arm higher. The left leg out a little more—"

"Walk me home?" Willow asked Xander at the gate to the school grounds.

Xander shrugged his shoulders and said, "Sure. Why not? Why does Giles insist on giving Buffy combat lessons?" he asked, casually. "She keeps mopping up the floor with him."

"Somebody has to do it, I suppose," Willow replied. "Maybe Giles just wants her to keep her edge."

"Yoo-hoo! Yoo-hoo!" called out a woman's voice from a street to their left.

Willow and Xander turned to see a man and woman getting out of a gigantic Hummer with tires that looked big and wide enough to ride the surface of Mars, if need be.

The man was in his mid-forties and wore an ill-fitting designer suit; he was just now getting out of the driver's side. The woman, who was about a decade younger than he, wore a stylish, modern, blue power jacket and skirt. She'd been so intent upon reaching Willow and Xander she had left the passenger door open for the man to close. "Kids! You go to Sunnydale High, don't you? May we have a word with you?" she called out insistently.

"I bet I know what she wants to find out," whispered Willow.

"This is too weird," said Xander.

"Thank you, this will just take a few moments. My name is Lora Church," she said, holding out her hand. Her hair was short and brown, her face round, attractive and cheerful. "This is my husband, Rick. Your name is Willow, am I right? And you must be Xander?"

"Yeah, how did you know?" asked Xander, who found it somewhat difficult to take his eyes off her.

Willow nodded suspiciously. She didn't like it when Xander noticed beautiful strangers, be they from afar or close-up. But then Rick Church looked into her eyes and she found herself holding her breath.

Managing to possess the illusion of danger while acting like a perfect gentleman, Rick Church said, "Well, Xander, we have a mutual acquaintance. She suggested you and your beautiful young friend here might be able to fill us in on the many unusual occurrences in Sunnydale."

"Really!" said Xander dryly. "Actually, it's not the number of occurrences but the lack of them that I find the most interesting. Nothing ever happens in Sunnydale. People don't even run red lights here."

"So who's our mutual acquaintance?" asked Willow.

"A ghost," said Rick. "You don't really know her, though she knows very well who you are."

"Explain," said Willow simply.

"On those nights when there really isn't a whole lot to do, my husband and I hold séances," said Lora. "We call up dead acquaintances or family members, just to see how they're getting along in the afterlife. Or we call up historic figures at random. We think of our séances as spiritual fishing expeditions. We've been pretty lucky. We've spoken to the spirits of Cleopatra, Alexander the Great, Victor Hugo."

"All in English?" asked Xander.

Rick laughed weakly and looked at Willow as if she were the only woman in the entire world. "It's been well documented that called-up spirits tend to speak in the language of the séance holders, whose minds they must be filtered through. Well, last week, we bumped into someone who claimed to have been reborn and living in Sunnydale."

"If the spirit was reborn, then how come you reached it on the astral plane?" asked Willow immediately.

Rich blinked; he hadn't been expecting that question. "Why indeed? But who else could be in two places at the same time, if not a spirit? This spirit distinctly mentioned you, young lady."

"What did she say?" asked Willow.

"Not much," said Lora. "Spirits rarely do. She intimated that the two of you have a lot in common with us, and suggested—most strongly—that we look you up."

"Which we did," said Rick. "So what do you think of that, Willow? Your fame precedes you."

Willow had the distinct feeling this charming man was an utter fruitcake. "Gee, I'm flattered but, hey, I told my mother I would help around the house after school. We can talk later."

"Fair enough," said Rick. "When? Soon, I hope. Surely it shouldn't be too much trouble to fit in a cup of coffee—or a milk shake—with Rick and Lora Church, occult mavens extraordinaire." He bowed slightly, gallantly. "You might have the rare opportunity to take part in one of our supernatural adventures."

Willow decided that in the final analysis, the fruitcake was still charming. "How about tomorrow," she suggested.

"Excellent! Same time, same place? I trust that will give you enough time to do a background check on us via the World Wide Web?"

Willow grinned. "Plenty of time. I mean, uh, that'll be fine. C'mon Xander, we've gotta go."

Xander still couldn't take his eyes off Lora. So Willow took him by the arm and pulled him away. Lora and Rick waved good-bye at them.

"By the way," called out Lora, "where can we find Rupert Giles?"

"In the library. Where else?" Xander replied, flattered to have been asked.

"Xander!" Willow hissed.

"Oops. Sorry."

They walked. Willow was relieved to be alone again with Xander, but it still bothered her that the Church couple had asked for Giles. Considering everything that was going down, perhaps she should have been more curious.

Lora Church and her husband opened the library doors the instant Giles flew out—backwards! He missed them both completely, landing rump-first on the hard tile floor. Lora grimaced at the impact. "Ooh! That had to hurt!" Rick said.

"Ouch!" was all Giles said after hitting the floor. He didn't have time to say anything else, because he was still sliding across the hall.

From inside the library, Buffy shrieked at what she'd done, and she ran into the hall, between Rick and Lora, without noticing them.

They realized immediately this lithe, slip of a girl was responsible for the commotion. "Hey! Wait up!" Rick cried out, as he and Lora followed Buffy to where Giles lay, unconscious and unmoving, except for a few twitches now and again.

Buffy knelt beside him and felt his pulse, then she put her ear to his chest. "Come on, Giles, I know you're alive," she said, "I can hear you wheezing."

"Wait, wait, young lady, I know first aid," said Rick, gently pushing her aside. He had already taken off his jacket and was putting it gently under Giles's head. "Giles. Giles! Are you comfortable?"

Giles shook away three or four of the zillion cobwebs clogging his brain. "I make a pretty good living," he croaked. Then he groaned. "I need a cup of instant coffee." Suddenly, he woke up, getting his bearings instantly. He looked at them all suspiciously. "Who are you?" he demanded.

"I'm Buffy." She peered closely at Giles, trying to determine whether he really didn't remember her.

"I know that! I'm talking to *him!*"

Rick bowed his head slightly. "Rick Church,

pleased to make your acquaintance, sir, and this is my wife—"

Giles gasped. Suddenly he had recognized her . . . from somewhere. A few seconds passed. He gasped again. "Lora—?"

"You know each other—?" said Rick in surprise.

"Hello, Rupert," Lora said. "It's been a long time."

"Hello, Lora," said Giles, his eyes going all misty and sentimental. "Nice to see you."

Xander listened; Willow talked. It was a sunny afternoon, the air was warm and exhilarating, and he could barely keep his mind on what Willow was saying.

Eventually he concentrated hard enough to gather that her computer had crashed the night before and she'd stayed up till three fixing it. Willow detailed every method she'd used to find out which program had corrupted the others as if Xander should have been fascinated by the process. As it was, he could barely understand. . . .

What a second! Xander thought. *Normally I'm only too happy to listen to Willow. But something's calling me, like a songbird from over the next hill. . . .*

Then he heard it: the sharp *crrrack!* of a bat striking a baseball dead-on, and the cries and cheers of young boys playing around the next corner. Willow was three steps behind before she realized he'd sped up.

"Sorry, Willow, I know I promised to walk you home, but I just realized—"

"Oh." She was none too successful at hiding her disappointment, but it didn't matter because Xander didn't notice. "What's that?"

"It's spring, and in spring, a young man's fancy turns toward—"

"Yes?"

"Baseball."

"Oh."

"See ya!"

The sandlot game was in its fourth inning when Xander asked to join one of the teams. Xander couldn't hit the broad side of a barn with a baseball from a yard away, but one team needed a right-fielder—the position least likely to see any action, making it the position for which Xander was most perfectly suited.

Willow watched Xander play until it became apparent Xander would ignore her completely, because that's how boys were supposed to treat girls when they were playing baseball.

So she walked a few blocks to a small park and sat down on a bench. She read Jane Austen's *Sense and Sensibility* until the game was over. Maybe then Xander would be interested in walking her the rest of the way home.

The distant noise of the game barely made a dent in her consciousness as she became lost in Austen's comedy of nineteenth-century English marriage, death and manners. She was jolted back to the present by the sudden knowledge that one of Xander's teammates—a huge blond with more muscles on his arms than she thought possible—was trying to get her attention.

"Earth to Willow! Come in please!"

"What—?"

"It's Xander! He's been hit on the head!"

"Oh no! Poor Xander! Is he hurt?"

"With him it's kinda hard to tell. A fly ball hit him on the head and knocked him out. He's been wacky ever since, calling your name, calling other people's names."

"Such as Mom? Dad? Giles? . . . Buffy?"

"No. He's talking about someone named John Kane. And who else? Danforth. Corwin. Ever hear of any of these people? 'Cause I sure haven't."

But Willow was already running away. She was out of breath and utterly exhausted by the time she reached right field. The two teams were gathered around Xander. One of the smaller guys poured water from a plastic bottle on his face. "Let him breathe! Let him breathe!" she yelled, despite her burning lungs.

The boys parted to let her through.

"Xander! Are you all right?"

Just then he woke up, sputtering water. "Willow! I just had the strangest dream!"

"Terrific—he's awake, folks!" shouted the short guy. "That's three outs!"

* * *

"It's good to meet you too," said Rick Church, shaking Giles's hand. "Although I must admit I'm surprised I hadn't heard about you until recently," he added, staring at his wife.

Buffy grinned at Giles's red-faced embarrassment.

"Mrs. Church and I were together on the Oxford debate team, Buffy," said Giles.

"And that was only the beginning!" said Lora happily.

Giles looked at Rick, directly and honestly. "Yes, but after we graduated we lost touch, as university teammates are so inclined to do."

"I never would have guessed," said Rick dryly.

Giles was escorting Buffy and the Churches into the library, then seemed to think better of it. "Would you care to join me for a cup of coffee in the teachers' lounge? I feel the need to freshen up."

"But what about me?" Buffy blurted out.

"I think the combat lesson is over for today," said Giles. "I've really had enough punishment."

"You're teaching *her* combat?" exclaimed Lora. "You *have* changed!"

Giles cleared his throat. "Not as much as you think. In the ways of combat, Buffy is the instructor, while I am just the pupil."

"She's teaching *you!*" Rick laughed

Buffy opened her mouth to reply, but Giles stifled her by putting a hand on her shoulder and steering her away, while saying to Rick, "She has a gift, remarkable for one so young. Now why don't you two wait for a moment? Buffy usually offers me a few private words of encouragement after my lesson, and today I desperately need to hear them."

Rick snickered. "Sure. We'll be right here." He watched them make a turn down another hall and then said to his wife, "What did you see in *him?*"

Lora smiled, remembering the young Giles fondly even as she said, "How am I supposed to know? I was young and impressionable. Besides, remember that truckstop waitress you told me about once? What did you see in her?"

"That was completely her idea. I had nothing to do with it."

"A likely story. Anyway, it doesn't matter. Since meeting you, I never thought of Giles at all until the ghost suggested we see him while we were in Sunnydale."

"Now I'm happy." He pointed at his lips. "How about another smooch?"

Meanwhile, Buffy was letting loose with a barrage of questions about Giles's personal life. And even though Giles tried to impress Buffy with the fact that his pre-Watcher existence was none of her business, he nonetheless couldn't help remarking, "It's like seeing a ghost, only I've seen ghosts and they're not nearly as attractive. She has such wonderful—" He cleared his throat. "Buffy, I have no idea what Lora and this Rick Church fellow—"

"Her husband," Buffy pointed out.

"—are doing here, but I will find out. I wouldn't

be surprised if it has something to do with the Eisenberg prophecy."

"Why? Maybe she and her husband are just passing through town."

"I suspect this ghost they spoke of is helping them overcome the spell of forgetfulness too. Besides, did you notice something profound about the connection between Lora and me? I think you would call it 'cosmic.'"

"Why would I do that?"

"It wasn't quite as if we were actually destined for one another, like genuine soul mates, just that we shared the feeling we'd shared something, sometime, somewhere, where there was a place for us. Then, for no apparent reason, we drifted apart. But it's gratifying to know something of that feeling remains to this day."

"I don't call that 'cosmic.' It's more like *Cosmopolitan*."

"I wonder what she wants."

"Now that's the suspicious Giles I know," said Buffy, already walking away.

He frowned as he watched her go. *I'm not just suspicious of women,* he thought defensively, *I'm suspicious of everyone!*

With a sharp intake of breath he realized that he was even suspicious of his dreams. Although it behooved a Watcher to be paranoid, he couldn't help wondering if he was going too far.

But when he returned to Rick and Lora in the hall, they'd been having an intense discussion that ceased the instant he walked in. "Well, Lora, this is certainly a pleasant surprise, but you didn't come all the way to Sunnydale from wherever it is you're living now—"

"Carmel," she put in helpfully.

"—just to look me up," Giles continued.

"I should hope not," said Rick slyly.

"The teacher's lounge is that way," said Giles. "We'll probably have more privacy there."

On the way, he and Lora tried to catch up with one another. Twice Lora mentioned her surprise that he had not been married, not even once, during the last two decades. Rick remarked that he'd been married and divorced enough times for all three of them.

"You must be rich," said Giles.

"Not anymore," said Rick.

Inside the lounge, Giles led his guests to a corner furnished with pieces purchased from the Salvation Army. "So really, people, why are you here?"

Rick and Lora suddenly became quite serious. "A ghost named Sarah Dinsdale suggested we come see you," said Rick.

CHAPTER 5

By the time she turned on to her block, Buffy felt pretty good inside, thanks in part to her plan to take a nap as soon as she made it home in the hopes of learning about the fate of Samantha Kane.

Suddenly her good feeling evaporated. What was that huge van with the satellite dish on top doing across the street from her house?

On both sides of the van was painted a large, garish logo: a column of frogs falling from a clear blue sky. Buffy recognized it as the hallmark of the syndicated show dealing with paranormal phenomena called *Charles Fort's Peculiar Planet*. It aired on Channel 13, appropriately enough, every weeknight at 11 P.M. The subject matter ranged from giant ants in the Amazon to the ghosts of aliens on the space shuttle. Buffy usually watched it for laughs, but she wasn't laughing now.

Especially when the show's top reporter, Eric Frank, got out of the passenger side and, microphone in hand, headed toward her front door!

"Sarah Dinsdale, eh? Never heard of her." Giles sipped his cup of coffee. Today the coffee machine in the teachers' lounge was producing an especially bitter product, and he fought to maintain a neutral expression lest the Churches think he was uncomfortable with the subject matter. He had played dumb for a while, a skill he'd picked up through necessity while dealing with the education bureaucracy on both sides of the Atlantic.

"Funny," said Rick, with a smile. "She seems to have heard of you." He sipped his coffee and immediately stopped smiling.

"I don't see how," Giles replied casually.

"Oh please, Giles," said Lora impatiently. "You were always interested in the occult. It's all you ever talked about."

"I'm afraid you have me confused with someone else," said Giles indignantly. "I'm interested in books and movies and art."

"Humph! You never had time to see any movies unless they starred Christopher Lee or Peter Cushing," said Lora.

"Do I detect a trace of resentment?" chuckled Rick.

"Sweetums," Lora cooed. Nevertheless she continued the attack on Giles. "The only books you ever read had to do with paranormal subjects such as spontaneous combustion and psychic detectives—and the art, good grief, the art! It was all primitive stuff and usually had been handled by witch doctors first."

"Ever do any research on UFOs?" Giles asked in all innocence.

"Don't change the subject," said Lora. "The ghost of Sarah Dinsdale sent us to see you. And that's why we're here."

Giles sighed. He'd forgotten how stubborn Lora could be when she felt like it. But that was part of the problem. Over the years, he'd forgotten almost everything about her, but now that she was in his presence again, memories and emotions were resurfacing like salmon jumping up a waterfall.

"All right," said Giles. "What does this Sarah Dinsdale want with me?"

"I'm glad you asked!" said Rick briskly, his eyes darting this way and that. He lowered his voice. "Is this place bugged?"

"I should certainly hope not!" said Giles, hoping he was right.

"Good. What I am about to tell you, most people would find somewhat extravagant—perhaps unbelievable. But I assure you, every word is true."

"Or close to it," added Lora.

"Lora and I used to look forward to our weekly séances, when we'd sit in our darkened den to call forth the spirits of the dead."

"There were no portents the night Sarah came—subjective or otherwise—that the upcoming séance would contain a few unpleasant surprises," said Lora.

"No sudden flashes of lightning in a clear sky," said Rick. "No white owls in the trees, not even an old-fashioned chill up the spine. I had my hopes, too. Cleopatra had intimated she'd be back for a return engagement, and lately we'd snared a few ladies-in-waiting from the court of King Louis XVI of France."

"Those weren't ladies," said Lora. "I myself was hoping Nijinsky, the great ballet dancer, would drop in again, though in a mood less neurotic than before."

"You just like what you see in his eyes," said Rick jealously.

"You just like Cleopatra's—" Lora began, before Giles interrupted and reminded them of the story they were supposed to be telling. "Of course," said Lora. "You can imagine our surprise when, having done this hundreds of times before, the séance conjured up all sorts of atmospheric effects, such as flickering candlelight, creeping fog and a stench so repulsive I won't begin to describe it to you."

"I have no problem doing that," said Rick. "It smelled like a thousand dead skunks piled on top of one another, lying on a bed of liver and castor oil. We couldn't have failed to notice it if we'd tried."

"I got ill," said Lora.

"Big time," said Rick, deliberately. "Luckily, I'd taken an antacid before dinner—for my ulcer, you know. When the ghost of Sarah Dinsdale appeared above us, we couldn't have been less in the mood for occult explorations. But there she was, nonetheless."

"She was the scariest ghost I've ever seen," said Lora. "Most ghosts are pretty alienated from reality to begin with—they say purgatory gets on a specter's nerves—but this one was frightening, paranoid and utterly confident in her spectral dignity. You never knew how she'd respond to any one of your questions."

"She blamed the smell on us, too," said Rick resentfully. "Said we weren't conjuring her up correctly. I took umbrage at that. "

"It wasn't long before she began asking *us* questions," said Lora. "And she insisted on answers! Threatened to go back if we didn't talk. Well, you never let a specter go away if you could help it. It just isn't done in polite society."

"Of course," said Giles. "What did she want to know?"

"Where you were," said Lora. "How you were faring on this mortal coil. Things of that nature."

"I had never heard of you, of course," said Rick.

"What did she say, exactly?" asked Giles impatiently.

Lora answered, "She said you had a good head on your shoulders. But then she implied you'd lost it before and that you might again if you weren't careful."

"This is all very interesting," he said guardedly, "but how seriously am I supposed to take this warning? Especially since I never heard of the ghost before and have no idea what she could possibly be talking about."

"This is not the first time we've heard a dire warning or received a vague, almost nonsensical clue that's required action on our part," said Rick. "In the past, we've solved murders long set aside by the authorities. We've also added significantly to our stock portfolio by taking advantage of what spirits have told us about the immediate future. It all depends on the situation."

"We don't know exactly what Dinsdale was talking about," said Lora, "so we don't really know what we might have to do. But when the clutch comes, we'll be there for you."

"Yes. Well, ah, thank you, but that won't be necessary," said Giles. "I may seem a little awkward occasionally, but I think I can take care of myself."

"So long as you don't have to fight any teenage girls," said Rick with a smirk.

"Buffy is not just a teenage girl, she's—" Giles caught himself; he'd almost let his pride cause him to spill the beans. "She's a black belt, a gifted brawler in the most profound sense of the word."

"She can't guard you as well as we can," said Rick.

"I've no doubt whatsoever, but I feel pretty safe," said Giles, which was definitely untrue, but he had to maintain a facade of not taking them seriously. "Besides, there are times when—*ahem*—a man must do what a man must do, and I'd rather be by myself when I do them."

"We're still going to be close by," insisted Rick. "We're very good at this bodyguard thing. We've had lots of practice."

"Ever lose any of your charges?' Giles asked.

"We don't talk about that," said Lora tensely. "There were extenuating circumstances. How were we to know there'd be a killer shark in that lake?"

"Our failures have been few and far between," Rick said. "Barely worth mentioning, in fact."

"Well, I feel safer already," said Giles. He sipped his lousy coffee, barely noticing the taste. He suppressed the sudden urge to excuse himself and go home for a nice, long nap.

"Sorry I left you for a baseball game," said a still-woozy Xander as Willow walked him home. "I just wanted to be a *manly* man."

"And *baseball* is the way to prove your manliness?" asked Willow, clearly confused at his logic.

"Yeah. You know what it's like to be one of the few who can actually remember all the strange doings in Sunnydale, to know you've performed some pretty brave—"

"Or foolhardy," interjected Willow.

"—actions, and to want everyone to know about

everything: the doings and the actions. But you can't, so you'd settle for just being a normal person who can do normal things like playing baseball—"

"Or having a girlfriend," said Willow, leading him on although she knew in advance it wouldn't do any good.

"You want a girlfriend?" Xander asked, surprised.

"Never mind. Tell me about your strange dream."

Xander cleared his throat. "Well, to begin with, it seemed so real. I feel like I can recall every detail. But that wasn't the strangest part."

"Go on."

"Remember Giles's dream that took place in the seventeenth-century Massachusettes Bay Colony? Mine appeared to happen at roughly the same time. But even that wasn't the strangest part."

"Xander, get to the point."

"It's embarrassing. I dreamed I was a girl. Or rather, a woman. A full-grown adult woman."

"I always knew you had a feminine side," said Willow, smiling.

"*I* didn't!" Xander exclaimed.

"Boys rarely do. Perhaps you should tell me exactly what happened."

They sat down on a bus stop bench and he began talking. At first he was reluctant, but as he got going, he couldn't help himself. Besides, if he couldn't trust Willow with the dream then who could he trust?

At first the dream was like all dreams—a series of mixed-up images, half-profound, half-absurd. All the images resonated with the power of real life, only they had little to do with the experiences of a teenage boy growing up in sunny Southern California. They had more to do with the experience of growing up a young girl in seventeenth-century New England.

The images included reading the Bible at home, feeding the farm animals, growing the vegetables and going to church. Apparently the young girl went to church quite frequently, as did practically everyone else in the vicinity. Only she didn't like it.

This is where the images took on a different character. Before, everything was bathed in light. Now the dream settings became rather dark— more pleasant, ocasionally, but always dark. During these parts of the dream, the young woman felt much more free, as if she was finally in control of her life after a long period of imprisonment. Xander tried not to exert his will or even his thoughts. He just let the dream unfold.

The images included several of walking through a forest of exquisite, pristine greenery teeming with everything from huge colonies of insects to squirrels, skunks and hedgehogs. The bears and wildcats, Xander somehow knew, had been pushed out of the vicinity by the Puritans some time ago, though of course a few always ventured into the farmlands hunting for sheep and goat.

The young woman walked through fields of purple wildflowers. She harvested wild mushrooms and dug up mandrake roots in the forest. She searched for stones and metals by the streams. She slew frogs and mummified them, and then she went into caves and slew bats. Those were mummified, too, according to ritual with the muttering of spells and chants.

The young woman traveled to these places during both day and night, but she especially enjoyed those nights when she was alone. It was then that she danced beneath the moon, communing with nature on a level so primitive and barbaric it horrified Xander.

Finally the dream returned again and again to those times the young woman spent at church, concentrating on the appearance—but never the words, apparently—of the charismatic young preacher, John Goodman. She saw in him potential that she saw in no other man, the potential to be a worthy life-partner in marriage.

Of course, they were apt to disagree over what type of marriage ceremony might be appropriate.

By now the bond between Xander and his dream alter ego was so strong Xander didn't know where he ended and she began. Conversations, memories, books read—it all blended together. Xander was becoming a new person. In a new time.

Xander knew exactly when and where he was: in Salem, Massachusetts, in 1692. His name in the dream was Sarah Dinsdale, and she was most definitely a witch. Up until a certain point she had avoided being victimized by the hysteria—which was ironic, because while she was fairly convinced most of those accused were innocent, she herself was *guilty, guilty, guilty*.

It was a situation that Sarah must have felt inevitable, because she was strangely calm when the church scenes faded out and the courtroom sequence faded in. She stood in chains in the square pen the courtroom reserved for the accused; a large orange "W" was sewn on her dress.

The stern, robed Judge Danforth regarded her severely. Nine angry men sat in the jury box. Sheriff Corwin stood in the back of the courtroom. Cotton Mather, the famed scholar and witch hunter from Boston, stood at the prosecutor's table asking questions of a pale, nervous John Goodman, who sat fidgeting in the witness chair.

The first question Mather directed at Goodman was, "And when did you first hear the unholy call of this Sarah Dinsdale?" His words echoed in Xander's mind like reverb at a rock concert.

Sarah Dinsdale suddenly shouted, "I object, your honor! That question is prejudicial and implies I have already been found guilty!"

The people in the court were shocked—she had dared to speak without the permission of the court! Sheriff Corwin grumbled something about Sarah being mighty darn guilty in his opinion.

Judge Danforth glared down sternly at Sarah Dinsdale. "Nothing would please me more if you were found to be innocent of those crimes of which you stand accused," he said, his tone belying his words. "But do not forget you are forbidden to speak, woman. You would do well to be silent, lest the crime of casting a spell on a member of the court is added to your long list of crimes."

"What do you mean by 'prejudicial'?" Mather inquired, idly scratching beneath his wig.

Judge Danforth seemed satisfied with Sarah's silence. He gestured for Goodman to break his. Goodman cleared his throat, apparently with some difficulty because he took quite a while doing it. Meanwhile, Mather folded his arms and drew himself to his full height. He had been waiting for this moment for some time and was impatient with Goodman's delay.

Finally Judge Danforth cleared his throat. Loudly. He and Goodman looked one another in the eye, and suddenly Goodman knew what to do.

He spoke. "It was during winter," he began softly, "and I was thinking of the pagan holiday then being observed by those citizens of the Old World, the very ones who persecuted we Puritans for not practicing religion properly. I happened to be walking by the modest home of Goodwoman Dinsdale. And I confess, I did think about her of my own free will."

"And what exactly," asked Mather, "did you think about her?"

"I thought it odd that such a pleasant young

woman, so lovely and so hard-working, so obviously capable of running a household, was unwed. And at her age too."

"One might say the same about you, sir Goodman," said Mather easily. A few women in the courtroom giggled, but Judge Danforth's stern look quickly put a stop to that.

Goodman blushed, and this pleased Sarah Dinsdale, although at the moment things did not look promising between them. "In any case, passing by Miss Dinsdale's house, I perceived the distinct odor of mincemeat pie."

The audience gasped. It was forbidden to bake mincemeat pie in the winter, because in Europe the baking of mincemeat pie was a major part of celebrating Christmas, which Puritans believed was a pagan holiday.

"I knocked upon her door, and when she opened it to greet her guest, I pushed my way in. And that was when I saw, much to my chagrin, that Sarah Dinsdale was already among the damned."

"I see, my son," Mather said almost tenderly. "Then what course of action did you take?"

"The only one available. I denounced her. I had no choice. For in her kitchen I saw mummified bats and parts of frogs. I saw roots and other ingredients from the recipes of Old Scratch himself! I knew then and there she was unclean—that she was a witch!"

"A witch! A witch!" shouted many in the court, until Judge Danforth's threat brought a renewed sense of order to the proceedings. During that time Goodman could not look Sarah in the eyes, but she could look in his. And she liked what she saw there.

For there was no hate and no pity in John Goodman's eyes. There was only guilt—guilt that he was the one who had been forced—in his view—to denounce her.

"Since then, knowing she is a witch has made no difference. I cannot get the heinous female out of my mind. She haunts my dreams, she occupies my every waking thought. Surely she has cast a spell on me; she has looked upon me with her evil eye and devoured my soul."

Sarah could not resist a smile. Hearing those words had made worthwhile all the suffering she'd endured the past few weeks in the witch dungeons controlled by Sheriff Corwin.

Sarah was still smiling, inwardly at least, when the scene shifted slightly and Xander heard and saw, through her eyes, Judge Danforth pronouncing the death sentence: she will hang by the neck until she is dead! Sarah was confident this would never happen, even when Judge Danforth remarked that he would like to see Old Scratch save her now.

"Not Old Scratch," said Sarah. "Just a close personal friend."

The people in the court erupted with shouts of shock and anger. Sarah surveyed them with a regal, contemptuous air, and Xander couldn't help wondering if it was true that if you dream of your death, then you really die. He was afraid he would find out when the scene next shifted. . . .

. . . Only instead of cutting to the gallows, the scene cut to Sarah Dinsdale sitting contentedly in her dungeon cell, chained to the wall. A visitor arrived, sitting down on a three-legged stool on the other side of the bars.

It was John Goodman.

It was obvious he was coming as close to her as he dared. He fidgeted nervously and couldn't find a comfortable way to sit. He clearly wished he was anyplace else but here within these cold, damp stone walls, which were stained with the blood of accused witches who had confessed upon pain of torture; presumably the poor women had already gone on to receive their "just rewards."

Sarah, for her part, couldn't make up her mind how she felt about John Goodman's appearance here. She knew she should hate him. But his reaction to seeing her prepare her witch's stock had only been true to his nature, and even now something in his eyes reminded her why she'd desired his attention in the first place.

"I've come to say good-bye," Goodman finally said, softly.

"Are you certain you haven't offered me one last chance at redemption?" said Sarah defiantly.

"You should repent," said Goodman flatly.

"Why? To ease your guilty conscience?"

"I did not choose these feelings I have toward

you, Sarah Dinsdale. I do not hold myself responsible."

"Then who is responsible for them?"

"I think you are."

"It is true I cast a spell over you, Reverend John Goodman. But my spells are too weak to last this long. Perhaps my spell merely revealed an emotion that was already there."

Goodman's complexion wavered between becoming red with anger and pale with fear. He smashed his fist against the bars of Sarah's cell. "That is impossible! I could not—cannot have these feelings toward a proven witch of my own volition! Release me from this curse! I beseech you!"

Sarah threw back her head and laughed. She also bumped her head against the stone wall, but she tried to hide that and concentrate on her laughter instead. "My most profound apologies, Reverend, but I can no more release you from your heart than I can free you from your conscience."

Goodman stood and nodded grimly. "Then that is how it must be. You are damned. I pity thee."

"I have never knowingly harmed another. I have used my powers only for good, only to help others. How then can I be damned?"

"Because your powers are derived from Old Scratch, and He corrupts all good that He touches."

"There are many ways to be damned, John

Goodman, as I suspect you are about to find out." She grinned, wickedly. At the moment she had no doubt which of the emotions she felt toward Goodman was dominant. "Perhaps there is a last wish I may grant you before I go forth to be damned."

"I would"—he cleared his throat—"appreciate it greatly if you would cease visiting my dreams, so that I may sleep in peace."

Sarah laughed again; never had she tasted a victory so sweet. "There are things not even a witch can do."

"May you face your death bravely," said Goodman as he turned to leave.

"The least of my worries," said Sarah casually, as the scene shifted slightly and a rat sniffed about on the stool where Goodman had been. Sarah, still chained against the wall, looked down at her feet where several other rats sniffed about. She was not afraid of the rats. Their presence here meant she was no longer alone.

Through the bars she could see the moon setting in the sky; it would be dawn soon. A terrible stench permeated the air. Things became damp with the coming of the early morning fog. A wolf howled, an owl hooted, someone in an adjoining cell screamed. Two of the rats began fighting over a discarded piece of bread.

Through it all, Sarah felt relieved. Help was on the way. He did not disappoint her.

She just saw his face for an instant, a flash from a reality whose existence she could barely grasp. She sensed the face's terrible green complexion, its horrible fangs, its dead, remorseless eyes—eyes somehow capable of peering into the deepest reaches of her soul.

She liked feeling exposed that way. How could she fail to trust the Despised One?

The scene in the dream shifted again, to when Sarah had already escaped and was running through the forest. The forest was pitch-black, clouds hid the moon, and the ground was covered with bush and thicket, yet Sarah made her way with ease, as if she was doing nothing more difficult than navigating through her own house in the dark.

She was exhausted. All she wanted was to lie down on the cold earth and sleep.

But if she did that, then she might as well give up and die, and she could not do that. Not while the Despised One was waiting.

She ran to him, deeper, deeper into the forest until she vanished in the night and Xander woke, returning at last to his own reality. The dream had seemed like a four-hour epic on television, yet he awoke to find he'd only been out for as long as an extended commercial break.

Upon hearing the full story, an awe-struck Willow discovered she was practically speechless—emphasis on *practically*. "My goodness, do you realize that your dream and the one Giles said he had both took place during the Salem witch trials?"

"I like to think mine was a little better. Yeah, and maybe they are connected. Even *I* can see that."

"We must find out more."

Xander yawned and stretched. "Yeah, I could use a nap. Maybe I'll dream the next part of the story. Should be easy enough, don't you think?"

"I have a better idea. What are you doing tonight?"

CHAPTER 6

"*I have often wondered,*" said the Master aloud—
to no one—"*what it is like to dream, or to sleep. Is
that the essence of humanity?*

"*Or perhaps I just want to eat, and drink. True, I
have feasted on human flesh and occasionally have
even devoured a human soul, but I wonder about
real food. Scrambled eggs, for instance. With
ketchup and maple syrup on top. Or a Virginia
ham. Or perhaps what I really want is a simple cup
of a tea. If I had a cup of tea, would my cares drift
away? After I consolidate my control of the surface,
one of my first acts will be to find out. Hey!
Minions!*"

The black things who were his minions scurried
around his feet. "*Master! Master!*" they said in

squeaky voices, not quite in unison. "Speak, speak! Instruct us, and we shall serve. We ask for nothing more."

The Master yawned. "Bring me the spirits!"

"YES MASTER! RIGHT AWAY MASTER YOU BETCHA MASTER," they said, then scattered immediately in all directions. A few even disappeared into the walls.

Moments passed. Or was it hours? The Master decided he didn't care. When time no longer matters, the amount of it is irrelevant as well.

The point was the spirits showed up. Alone, without a minion escort, which meant the minions were still looking for them. Typical. Two of the spirits emerged through a wall, another rose up from the floor, and the fourth descended from above. In this form they resembled black, semi-transparent shower curtains.

They hovered and merely listened to the Master's words; in this form they could do nothing else.

"The pieces of the puzzle are in place at last," said the Master. "All the planets, in all the upper and lower dimensional planes, are in proper alignment. The stars are positioned favorably. The fortune reading by candle wax went well, as did the readings by bone dice and tarot card. Only the reading by the spilled entrails of a small rat fared poorly. Even so, the situation is close enough for celestial work.

"Things could be better on the ground. It would

preferable if everyone involved was an actual reincarnation.

"But I am satisfied that by influencing the thoughts of four occult chasers, I have brought to Sunnydale"—he shuddered at the mere mention of such an innocuous, happy word—"proper temporary receptacles for you, the four souls who served the Despised One so poorly three hundred years ago. It would have been nice to rely on more proven talent, but you, Heather, have been adequately devious during the séances called by that amateur Church couple. A good beginning, a good beginning for you all.

"Remember, the entire point of this operation is its predictability. Soon the four of you will have the opportunity to correct the mistake you made over three hundred years ago. Were you capable of such things, I know you would be thrilled.

"Now, depart. Begone. Skedaddle! You know what to do. And when the time is right, you shall do it, or the suffering you have endured so far shall be but a prelude to the pure hell your existence will become."

And they were gone.

The Master was again alone. In time his minions would return and scurry around his feet, apologizing profusely for yet another failure on their part. It didn't matter. Soon he would never have to tolerate their ineptness again.

* * *

Buffy had spent the last thirty minutes waiting for Eric Frank and his crew to leave. But they were obviously too stubborn to leave.

Every once in a while Frank, the anchor man who often went out in the field to conduct the most sensational interviews, knocked on the front door. Each time he stalked back waving his arms about and shouting something at his crew . . . at the house . . . at the trees . . . at anything he happened to see. Maybe he thought someone was really at home and was just refusing to answer the door. But every week on this day Buffy's Mom took an invalid neighbor out for a drive, and Buffy didn't expect her home for another hour, at least.

Buffy had seen *Charles Fort's Peculiar World* many times, and she'd thought it was pretty stupid every time. Frank's dim-witted staff must have finally picked up shreds of information and fragments to learn there'd been some funny goings-on in Sunnydale. Paranormal goings-on. And they must have grasped that Buffy was the connecting thread, despite the spell of forgetfulness that had been cast over the town.

So if Frank interviewed her mom, he would ask her how she felt about her daughter being the Slayer for this generation. Then the footage would be broadcast on syndicated TV for the duration of cable—severely impairing Buffy's ability to have a normal life.

Eventually Buffy tried to think of ways to fool

the reporters into abandoning their stakeout. She reasoned she could ring them up on their cell phones, pretend to be a talent scout from CNN and send them off on a wild-goose chase. But that required knowing their number, which she did not.

She could get their number, but that would require going to a pay phone, finding their office and/or studio number and then getting into phone lies that could take all kinds of time and lead to all kinds of complications. Definitely not a good idea.

Now, if Willow were here she would whip out her trusty portable and hack via satellite into their e-mail in about thirty seconds. Unfortunately, Willow wasn't here, and she wouldn't be likely happening by unless Xander happened to drop off the face of the earth.

Then suddenly things changed. Buffy simply *had* to go inside to use the nearest-available facilities, and she was darned if she would let a bunch of TV clowns stop her. She figured they wouldn't get any usable footage on her, not if she walked straight in.

Besides, not one of their stories on vampires, wasp women and heap monsters had been remotely accurate. Why should they suddenly start being credible with Buffy Summers?

Eric Frank stood leaning against the back of the van, huffing and puffing about something, when he suddenly saw Buffy coming. He sprang into life.

"Guys! Guys!" he hissed, loud enough for the world to hear. "That's her kid! Maybe the brat will spill something!"

Buffy was so stunned she stopped in the middle of the street, forcing an oncoming car to swerve around her. *Spill something?* she thought. *I'm "her kid—the brat"? They must be here to think—ohmigosh!—Mom!*

Like a gigantic mother hen from a Japanese monster movie, Buffy strode boldly up to Frank, stuck her finger in his face and yelled, "What do you want with Mom? Get out of here! Leave her alone!"

Eric Frank's response was deliberate obtuseness. He put his microphone in Buffy's face. And he looked down that long, slim nose and asked, with snotty politeness, "Good afternoon, young lady. Might I inquire why you are so defensive? Does it have to do with your mother?"

"Defensive? What do you mean, defensive? Neither one of us has anything to be defensive about!"

"Ah, so you deny the obvious. So tell me, Miss Summers, what exactly is your mother's relationship with the supernatural? And why are you covering for her? Don't you understand she is involved with heinous forces of evil?"

"What are you talking about? What heinous forces? Look, why don't you ask her?" *Uh-oh.* She'd just realized: a) what she'd said, and b) who happened to be recording it for the gratification of millions. She smiled weakly at the crew.

"We tried to ask her, at the gallery," Frank explained in insincere tones. "But she refused to speak for the record. And when she spoke off the record, she politely but emphatically suggested our next destination. We think she's under the influence of an insidious art deco sculpture from the Bronx."

"What?"

"The Moonman. The famous sculpture by the modern Italian master V.V. Vivaldi, who died under mysterious circumstances during the fascist reign of Mussolini. I don't like it myself. According to the story, it wound up in Mussolini's possession, whereupon everything promptly went downhill for the Italian dictator. Of course he did choose the wrong side during World War II. Just before he was hanged by his angry subjects, Mussolini blamed his entire downfall on a curse placed on the Moonman by Vivaldi. And he was just the first."

"I suspected as much."

Frank turned away and then looked at her from the corner of his eye, like a huffy history teacher. "An art speculator snatched the statue from the hands of the American forces right after the war. He died, but not before he sold it to someone else, who died, who sold the statue to someone else, who died, who had willed it to someone else, who died . . . you get the idea."

"So what's Mom got to do with it?"

"The point is that a local art gallery, *managed*

by one Joyce Summers, is putting on a tiny exhibition concerning V.V. Vivaldi. This statue is cursed. Everyone who's owned it, or has been responsible for it, has died, usually before their time. Tell me, Miss, *ahem,* Buffy, I'll give you one last chance to come clean to our audience of millions of mild-mannered Americans. Is there something *you feel you must share* about Joyce Summers's—your mother's—extracurricular activities?"

Buffy bristled. "I beg your pardon?"

"So you're confirming your mother is under the insidious influence of Vivaldi's infamous Moonman?" Frank asked, pushing it.

"Hey, Frank, why do they call it the Moonman?" the soundman asked snidely.

"It's not actually from our moon, is it?" asked the cameraman, just as snidely. Buffy got the impression those two's opinion of the show was about as high as hers.

"Vivaldi thought it was," Eric Frank said in exasperated tones.

"Hey! Why don't we put it on the show?" asked the soundman, laughing.

"Are you guys always this wrong about everything?" Buffy demanded, staking her entire credibility on her ability to be as off-base as possible. "I think you are. I've seen your show. To be honest, Mr. Frank, it's pretty preposterous stuff."

Eric Frank turned quite pale and glared at his

crew, who were laughing at him. "You don't trust me because of the way my hair looks, right?"

Buffy tried not to laugh. "Exactly," she said sympathetically. She pushed her way between Frank and his crew. "I'm sorry, boys, but I really gotta go!"

The crew laughed some more, but suddenly they spotted something and became totally serious. "Hey, Mr. Murrow," said the soundman, facetiously referring to a legendary TV newsman from the 1950s. "Over there! In that Hummer!" He pointed toward the huge jeep. "It's Rick and Lora Church!"

"Hmmm. Looks to me like they're headed toward the gallery," said Buffy, even though the Churches were actually headed *away.*

She'd been counting on the probability that the three strangers to Sunnydale would be too unfamiliar with the streets to recognize that fact—a slight risk that proved justified when all three began loading the gear into the van in a bumbling, comical fashion. Within a few moments a very satisfied Buffy watched the van with the falling frogs logo disappear after the Churches.

Naturally she was very concerned that Mom had gotten herself involved with a cursed artifact of some sort, and under normal circumstances she would gone to the gallery immediately. But today circumstances were far from normal. Curses, dreams and coincidences were running amok in

Sunnydale, and she was certain they were connected to Prince Ashton Eisenberg's Prophecy of Dual Duels.

Only one man could help her fathom that connection.

Rupert Giles. She would have to see him.

In a few minutes.

CHAPTER 7

Giles laid down on a couch in the library and wiped a line of perspiration from his forehead with a handkerchief made damp from the number of times he'd used it during the past hour. Buffy and her friends had never seen him this casual before: the buttons of his shirt were undone, he'd kicked off his shoes, and his feet were on a table. Of course, at the moment he had a temperature of a hundred and one, and he had just taken a few aspirin to reduce the fever.

"We should get you to a hospital," said Buffy.

"It wouldn't do any good," said Giles. "My illness isn't medical, or I should say, isn't scientific in nature. No rational person can help me now."

"Thank goodness," said Xander. "That means we might have a chance."

Giles coughed. "All right, the time has come for us to try to get this straight. Three of us—Buffy, Xander and myself—have had dreams linking us to past lives that all coexisted at the time of the Salem witch trials. We are not necessarily reincarnations, but all these past lives interacted with one another, much as all four of us interact today. The fact we are all having these dreams of the same people, the same events, at the same time is inescapable. There must be some significance, if not reincarnation then some joining of purpose. So let us, for the sake of argument, assume that we *are* them for right now."

"You are a Watcher named Robert Erwin, which stands to reason since you're a Watcher now," said Willow. "And Buffy is a Slayer named Samantha Kane."

"And I, for reasons I cannot possibly understand," said Xander, "have been dreaming that I was a woman named Sarah Dinsdale, a tried and convicted witch who just happened to be as guilty as sin."

"Furthermore," said Giles, coughing again, "because you are having the dreams of Sarah Dinsdale, we know the spirit Rick and Lora Church know as Sarah is likely the spirit of an imposter. Because the spirit of Sarah is within you, and can be nowhere else."

"So is this spirit in the employ of all the nosy people who've been bothering us?" asked Willow.

"Undoubtedly," said Giles. "But I suspect the nosy people are unwilling dupes."

"Obviously the next step is to learn more about what happened to Sarah Dinsdale," said Willow.

Xander stretched and yawned. "Great. I could use a few Z's. I've been told"—he looked at the girls meaningfully—"that I don't snore."

"Your teddy bear talks?" asked Willow.

"We do not have time to wait for you to dream," said Giles. "We must . . . how do you Americans say it? . . . cut to the quick on this one."

"I think you mean 'cut to the chase,'" said Buffy.

"Exactly," said Giles, suppressing another cough. "We must hold a séance. Willow, please retrieve the candles and the holy water from the locked cabinet behind the desk. Xander, on the shelf over there is a book called *Séances for Fun and Profit* by Rick and Lora Church. We need it. Buffy, I fear I must ask you to get something gross again."

Buffy gulped. "Okay."

Ten minutes later she returned from the morgue, with a vase filled with someone's ashes. "I suppose I'll have to take this back, too, in the morning."

"Hopefully, sooner," said Giles. "Thank you, Buffy. I must say, it always amazes me how you get in and out of these places so quickly."

"I could do it," said Xander, "if she could only show me how she does it."

"That's all right, Xander," Buffy said dryly. "I'll be glad to keep on doing it."

"I am grateful," said Giles. "Now in this book Lora describes the preparations for a do-it-at-home séance. She keeps it simple; the only exotic requirement is this demand for the ashes of the cremated. The curtains are drawn? Good. Now we must hold hands."

But he began coughing badly as he reached for Buffy and Willow. Everybody waited for him to be done. He sat at the head of the table, with Xander opposite him. The library was dark—Xander had switched off the lights—but for the candles, which were placed on the table to make the points of a pentagram, what Buffy called the occult design of choice. The wax formed the pentagram itself.

"I'll be fine," he said. "Obviously Robert Erwin had been very sick throughout the duration of this event, so obviously I'll be just as sick."

"What are you saying?" asked Xander.

"Merely that—*cough!*—what happened to our past lives during the event probably has . . . no, *must* have some bearing on what happens to us during this one."

"I get it," said Xander. "Like on television. Repeats always end the same."

"Once again, your logic is abnormal," said Giles. "But that is, in a roundabout way, the point."

"Well, this is one rerun where the ending's in doubt," said Buffy. "Whoever is setting up this repeat action must want a different ending, because there weren't any questions about a 'Depised One' on our history test today."

"Even so, if Sarah Dinsdale ends up being burned at the stake, I'm going to allow myself to feel very, very nervous, understand?" said Xander.

"The witches were hanged, not burned at the stake," said Giles. "We're not dealing with total barbarians here. The Puritans were as civilized as anyone else at the time. Furthermore, Sarah Dinsdale's name is not among the victims. She did not die as a witch."

"What happened to her?" asked Xander.

Giles shrugged. "After her escape, she disappeared. Whatever happened to her, her name is erased from history."

"That may be," said Buffy, "but from what I've seen, Corwin and Danforth weren't above extracting a little street justice."

Suddenly an incredibly bright light flashed from the nearby hills, followed not long afterward by a prolonged blast of thunder that rippled through the air.

"Funny, the weather babe said the skies would be clear all week," said Xander.

"I think we're about to experience an autumn New England storm," said Buffy. "The next time I sneak out, I'm grabbing some mittens."

"Let the séance begin," said Giles, controlling his cough as he and Xander took hold of the girls' hands. "This shouldn't be too difficult, since we know Sarah's spirit is already with us. We just have to bring it out."

The language recommended by the Church's book basically updated traditional séance chants. Since the spirits of the dead responded not to language but to the sentiment of the caller, how something was said wasn't nearly as important as *what* was said.

The Churches believed the "swami" of the séance should have all the slickness of the average infomercial host. Giles spent about twenty minutes laying down a sales rap to the spirit of Sarah Dinsdale, telling her it would be in her karmic self-interest if she revealed herself to the living.

Buffy, Xander and Willow concentrated with all their might.

Meanwhile, the rains came softly creeping in on the very fringes of their collective consciousness, which became stronger with every passing minute.

They felt no breeze, yet the candles flickered. Sometimes the flickering coincided with the thunder. Sometimes it coincided with the quivers up their spines.

The vases stood in the center of the pentagram. The participants in the séance tried to visualize the ashes inside, to imagine their texture, their smell, their taste.

Gradually the contents became easier to visualize. The energy passing between the four participants grew to a powerful current. The thunder overhead shook the entirety of Sunnydale High. Everyone's bodies felt lighter, but their minds became heavier. Forming thoughts was becoming more difficult as their content grew foggier. Meanwhile, Giles's voice droned on and on until it was just noise in the background.

Suddenly Xander stiffened, practically into a state of rigor mortis. Giles gasped and finally clammed up. Either at the same instant or a second later—Buffy couldn't be sure which—an incredible bolt of lightning struck a tree near the school with catastrophic force. A startled-out-of-her-wits Willow broke the chain with both hands, and Buffy listened detachedly to the wood and fire sizzling in the rain.

Buffy opened her mouth to say something when the thunder roared directly overhead; she couldn't even hear herself think, much less speak.

Xander, meanwhile, managed to remain stiff and to shiver as if he'd been dipped into ice water. He groaned. Willow leaned toward him, but Giles silently indicated she restrain herself. Which she did, but not without worry.

Buffy noticed the flash of light that had hit the vase inside the pentagram had yet to fade. If anything, it now glowed more intensely. Clearly the ashes of the dead had absorbed the magical energies released by the lightning bolt.

Outside, the rain slowly extinguished the fire. The lightning had sliced the trunk in half, and a column of ashes and smoke rose up from the wound. It was normal for the sidewalk and the road right outside Sunnydale High to be deserted this time of night—except when there were school activities such as ballgames and dances—but tonight the normal state of affairs seemed foreboding, as if reality itself was about to take a hike.

Xander already had, spiritually speaking. Buffy had been too busy concentrating on the subtle shift in the tone of their surroundings to notice that Xander had loosened up. Although still in a trance, he managed to stand of his own accord in a distinctive posture, with a definite personal body language.

Unfortunately, it was not his own.

It didn't take a rocket scientist to figure out who Xander was acting like. In Buffy's dreams Samantha Kane had yet to encounter Sarah Dinsdale, but the adventuress and the witch must have had a face-to-face at some point, because Buffy recognized Sarah with the gut-certainty of genuine memory.

Buffy's emotional reaction was the same as Kane's must have been too, because at that moment she hated the entity in Xander's body, loathed it with all her heart. She hissed and made a move toward Xander.

"Buffy! Xander is not an enemy!" hissed Giles. "He is merely possessed!"

"We better have him back when she's gone, otherwise Dinsdale's going to pay!"

"And how will you find me," asked Xander, "in this world or another?"

Gile's mouth dropped open. "Sarah Dinsdale?"

Xander shook his head as if to brush aside his hair. "At your service. I see I have been called. I'm not surprised. It was inevitable I would rank among the Summoned one day."

"You sound like you've been involved in séances before," said Willow.

Xander—or should we say—Sarah looked around at the library in wonder and spoke almost off-handedly. "Of course, but always one of the callers, never one of the called."

"Who have you called in the past?" Buffy demanded. "The Master?"

Sarah visibly deflated. "I have never heard of the Master. In my day I called, to my eternal shame, an evil entity known as the Depised One. My sole defense is that I was but a lonely, wayward mistress of the dark arts, and I had been told he would soothe my great loneliness."

"We need to know something," said Giles. "About you and Samantha Kane."

Outside it began to drizzle. Lightning flashed. The air in the library chilled.

Sarah hung her head in shame. "I understand. But what could you possibly want to know about Samantha Kane, other than I am the one primarily responsible for her death?"

Giles put himself between Buffy and Xander/Sarah. "Everything! It has been prophesied that tonight what has been done will be done again, and the official record is too sparse for us to prevent it from being done successfully this time."

"Ah, you speak of the prophecy. I did not realize the time had come."

"How do you know about Eisenberg's Prophecy?" Giles demanded.

Sarah looked at him as if he was truly naive. "We spirits have to know these things. Now I am truly glad that you called. I do not possess the means to help you in any material way, but I can provide you with information."

"That will be immensely helpful," said Giles. Outside, the drizzle had turned into a steady downpour. The fire had finally been extinguished, and a brisk, sustained wind began to build, shaking the trees and stirring the puddles.

"Why don't you start with what happened after you tried to kill Kane with that dead hand?" Buffy asked, with a sneer. She knew she should be more dispassionate, but she couldn't help herself.

"I had thought I had merely called up one corpse, that of a seaman who had died and been left there, long before, some time ago. But to my shame, I had not realized my ability to call forth the dead was beyond my control. I had inadvertently called up others—many others. Indians who had fallen from a white man's plague. Settlers who had died from a harsh winter and mothers who had died in childbirth. Souls not yet at rest."

"My grasp of the details is vague, because I was

not actually there and know only what other spirits have communicated to me. But I do know that the risen corpses found and attacked the vengeful ones from Salem seeking to recapture me."

"That's not in the history books!" exclaimed Willow.

Sarah smiled and shrugged. "Such incidents rarely are." Obviously whatever misfortune befell those men gave her pleasure, however much she may have suffered since.

Xander/Sarah walked to the window and looked outside. "Strange. I was making my way through the forest to a place feared and avoided by all savages, be they Puritan or Indian, when storm clouds rolled overhead and it began to rain, exactly as it is now.

"It was still raining when I finally reached my destination near the mouth of the Danvers River, not three hours before the dawn. At first I thought I was early, because the site was deserted. And it was not until I'd actually stepped foot on the site did I suspect all the ambitions and dreams of the last few years might have been part of some massive mistake on my part, for this place could not possibly have been prepared by men."

"How so?" Giles asked.

"Suddenly, with definite boundaries, the forest was clear-cut. Not even a stump remained where the great trees once stood. In their place stood thirty massive slabs roughly forming a horseshoe structure; more slabs lay on top of them, indicating either an entrance or a boundary—I did not know which.

"The slabs were gray, but they glowed with an incandescent blue neither the night nor the rain could dim. I knew, with the instinctive surety only one with my occult abilities could command, these slabs were not formed on Earth. But where? My wonderful instincts, I confess, did not provide me with a clue until I spied a small break in the storm clouds through which shone the light of the moon."

"They were moon rocks!" exclaimed Willow, "but how?"

"One small step for the Despised One," said Buffy, "one big bite for mankind."

"Certain meteors found in the Antarctic originated not from deep space, but from Mars," said Giles. "They were chunks knocked off the Red Planet with the impact of giant meteors. They spun around the solar system until they were captured by Earth's gravitational pull. Obviously the same thing could have happened with moon rocks."

Buffy immediately flashed on her vision of the moon being hit by exactly such a giant meteor . . . of a huge crater being formed, and of great slabs hurtling out into space.

Xander/Sarah walked back to his place at the table. Buffy noticed his hips moved with a distinct feminine rhythm. "I stood in the rain, cold, hungry and miserable, and waited. For the first time I wondered what I was doing there. At the moment I had no idea of the suffering my spell was causing, or of the fact that my body was already acting as the conduit for supernatural forces.

"As I waited there was little else for me to do but watch the storm. It was the most powerful I'd ever seen. Even the distant thunder was deafening, the distant lightning blinding. I wandered about aimlessly inside the rock edifice. I noticed the closer I walked to a slab—any slab—the more I felt strange energies stirring inside me.

"Suddenly I was struck straight on by a lightning blast. So great was its force I should have instantaneously burnt to a cinder. Yet, miraculously, I remained whole, bound by a blue light that held me high in the air like a fish caught in a net. I was immobile, and incapable of coherent thought.

"I could only watch helplessly as four people emerged from the forest at four different points before me, and I despaired at the extent of the trap that had been set for me—"

"How the mighty have pratfallen, eh, Sarah?" taunted Buffy.

Xander/Sarah whirled angrily at her and gestured. "Although my current male reincarnation is unpracticed in harnessing occult energies, I can still muster the strength to cast a terrible curse. I can smell the self-righteous smugness of the Slayer in you, girl."

"All right, stop it you two!" said Giles. "We must get to the bottom of this before we run out of time."

"Let me guess," said Buffy, "the four people were Cotton Mather, Judge Danforth, Sheriff Corwin and Hester Putnam."

"Yes, how did you know?"

"Slayer intuition."

"They were indifferent to me; I was no better than a wheat fetish or a berry potion in their eyes. Their talk revealed them at last as secret worshippers of the Despised One who had spent the past several months dutifully following his instructions, like the mindless sheep I'd always expected them to be. I just hadn't suspected the sheepdog would turn out to be the Despised One.

"Poor Cotton Mather actually thought his bargain with the Despised One would prove a boon for mankind. By sacrificing his soul to Old Scratch when he convicted the innocent of witchcraft, he hoped to turn others, many others, to the Good Word; and then the Almighty might forgive him and send his soul to Heaven.

"I truly believe that if the Despised One's plan had succeeded, poor Cotton Mather would have been among the first to be eaten."

"Cotton mouth," Buffy whispered aloud to no one in particular.

"I watched with wonder and horror as the four sheep performed the ceremony for calling forth the Despised One. It had never worked for me, but I'd always been alone. Alone, and manipulated. These people believed they were acting of their own free will.

"A multi-fingered fork of charged, white light struck the standing slabs in a sustained eruption. I twisted about in my blue prison and watched the archway of power reaching down from the sky like the wing of a great cathedral. This lightning did not die in an instant; rather, thanks to invisible sources of might, it was continuously renewed.

"Meanwhile, the storm intensified. The wind howled like anguished wolves. The rain came down in buckets, yet still could not extinguish the curious blue flames that had engulfed the slabs. The four worshippers held hands and performed a slow, unsavory dance. I felt their polluted souls rising above their bodies—I felt my mind's doors of perception widening in a manner I did not approve of. And all because of the power of that dance.

"I realized then that when it came to serving the needs of the Master, I was a rank neophyte. Surely he had thought me no better than a pawn, while these four were utter professionals.

"Suddenly they began to chant. A thousand invisible pinpricks skewered my body like so many thorns. My every nerve was in agony. Yet the cuts and bruises I had sustained during my flight healed completely. Even the scars that might have lingered disappeared. Indeed, the occult energies mended and cleansed my clothing as well. Obviously the

Despised One desired that his offering be presentable. But then my blood began to flow. I screamed; yet I heard no sound. This unholy place had rendered me silent."

"This is really exciting," whispered Willow to Buffy.

"Not when you consider that according to Eisenberg's Prophecy, this ceremony is going to be performed again, somehow," said Giles.

"Where's he going to get the moon rocks?" asked Willow.

"Yeah, Sunnydale is in the wrong part of the solar system to get moon rocks," said Buffy. Then she reconsidered. "Uh-oh. No, it isn't." She tapped the cover of her dream notebook.

"Will you people be quiet? Have all manners and propriety been lost in this future age?"

"Blame television," said Buffy. She happened to glance at the glowing vase as Sarah continued.

"The ground beneath the dancing fools transmuted as if by alchemy. Alternating between a bright crimson and a soft pink shade, it became translucent. From above I easily saw the flames of the underworld.

"The four worshippers brought their dance to a climax and fell to their knees. 'The Despised One comes!' they shouted in unison. 'Soon his presence shall be known to the entire world, and the entire world shall turn upside down!'

"The storm intensified to gale force. Trees fell

as if cut by an ax. The earth shook. The pale blue lightning became stronger, hotter, and the thunder even louder and more dissonant. Winged creatures with claw and fang flew in formation in the clouds.

"My thoughts sank in a chasm of helplessness. I believed the world wasn't turning upside down so much as it was dissolving in a pool of chaos.

"The worshippers rejoiced as suddenly a single, green, webbed hand protruded from the translucent, blood-red soil. The Despised One had arrived!

"Indeed—He had risen! He stepped up onto the solid earth as if he'd already conquered his greatest foe! Even from my distant vantage point, he was the ugliest creature I'd ever seen. His body looked like a cross between a dragon and a giant worm. His mouth was devoid of lips, and his nostrils were missing a nose. And those teeth! My arcane studies had informed me of a species of fish that lived in the southern hemisphere, a voracious, carnivorous fish with two rows of sharp, pointed teeth. These the Despised One's resembled.

"I could tell the entire world was going to be in for a cataclysm of biblical proportions, and there was nothing I could do about it. There was nothing anyone could do about it.

"Except for Samantha Kane. Surely her arrival could not have been as silent as it seemed. Doubtless the storm had concealed the sound of her horse's gallop. I am certain I was the first to spot her, and I trust my reaction was not so great that I inadvertently warned any of the others.

"In any case, they appeared most surprised when her horse bolted between them. Hester Putnam and Cotton Mather were knocked to the ground, while Sheriff Corwin and Judge Danforth were simply too stunned to react. I do not blame them. Had I been in their position, I would have been equally surprised.

"As Kane's horse galloped past the Despised One, she jumped from her saddle and threw herself directly on top of him. They both fell, but Kane fell on top. Keeping the startled Despised One pinned with her weight, she stabbed him with the hunting knife she held in one hand and poured holy water from the bottle she held in the other. She doused his face. Even in the rain and the confusion, I saw the steam rise from his head; I saw those terrible features disintegrate into a formless shape even more terrible; and I heard screams so horrible I would have felt pity had they come from anyone, or anything, else.

"The Depised One undoubtedly lacked the experience at physical combat that Kane demonstrated, but that did not prevent him from fighting back. The two fought furiously as they rolled in the mud, while the others, lackeys that they were, did nothing except look to one another for direction. In vain, of course.

"Then it was over: Kane had achieved victory. But at such a cost.

"For they both rolled into the transmuted ground an instant before it closed. Before they'd disappeared, I saw the Despised One sink his fangs into her shoulder and rip out a huge mouthful of flesh. Kane had surely been bleeding to death before the earth closed up around them."

"You don't seem exactly broken up about it," said Buffy.

"Why should I? Does she not live on in you, after a fashion?"

"As do you in Xander?" Willow asked Sarah.

"I stand corrected. The essence of Sarah Dinsdale indeed resides, temporarily, in this being called Alexander Harris, but I would not call it living. Even so, it is superior to being bound by the confines of nonexistence. I suppose you would like to hear, now, what happened after my occult prison disappeared and the four worshippers fled to resume their charades of respectability?"

"I'm not sure we have time," said Buffy, as an especially loud thunderclap resounded above the school. She noticed that the vase with the ashes inside was trembling, as if it and it alone were caught in an earthquake.

"I think we'd better get out of here," said Giles.

"Can't I just throw the vase in an open sewer or something, like in the movies?" Buffy asked.

Giles reached out to touch it, but drew his hand away before he actually did so. "Too hot."

"Darn," said Buffy, "and I'm all out of hand lotion. You're right. Ok, I'm outtie. Xander? Or should I say, Sarah? Are you with us?"

"All right, I've heard quite enough," someone said behind them.

Xander/Sarah was a little slow on the uptake, but the others all turned toward the person just in time to be blinded by a camera flash.

"MacGovern!" exclaimed Buffy, trying to blink away the spots in her eyes. "How long have you been standing there?"

"Long enough to learn that you four are part of a religious cult bent on world domination!" said MacGovern. His face was red and he was breathing hard. Buffy was about to protest when he flashed another picture, this one of Xander.

"What heinous sorcery is this?" Xander/Sarah cried, backing into a chair and falling down.

"It's the *science* of the fourth estate, young man, er, madam," replied MacGovern, both defiant and confused. "And now that I have my proof; the entire world will know what's going on in Sunnydale High Library!"

"No, you shouldn't report this!" Giles protested. "If people actually believe you, the media will keep her under constant surveillance!"

"Summers should have thought of that when she tried to take over the world!" MacGovern replied.

"Buffy! Quick!" said Willow. "Hit him over the head! Maybe it'll knock some sense in him!"

"It's too late for that!" said MacGovern, trying to get past them to the front door. "Stay away from me. It's my First Amendment right to be trespassing here!"

Suddenly the vase exploded. Everyone was inundated with ashes. Everybody was immediately grossed out, too—everybody except MacGovern, that is. He was inundated with one of the four blue shower-curtainesque fields of ectoplasm revealed in the aftermath of the explosion. The blue field outlined his body until it was completely absorbed. The others did not notice because they were still grossed out, and because the effect was disguised by the brilliant flashing of another lightning blast striking the school grounds. This time they heard the distinct sound of a wall crumbling.

"We've been undone!" Giles exclaimed, staggering backward onto a couch as if felled by a hammer. Already the perspiration brought on by his fever caused the ashes to run down his face. He looked like a crying clown with too many eyes.

"What makes you say that?" asked Willow. "Is it your fever?"

"Has something happened we should know about?" asked Buffy, who was always a little suspicious of Giles's tendency to withhold information until the last possible moment.

"I believe so," said Giles. "Whoever's manipulating present events to fulfill the prophecy of the Dual Duel used the mystical forces focused on the vase during our séance to pry open a gateway between the dimensions of the living and the dead."

"You know, it always amazes me that you're able to say so much without taking a breath," commented Xander.

If Willow tried to contain her excitement, it was lost on the others. She did restrain herself from throwing her arms around Xander, though just barely. "You're . . . yourself again!"

"Who else?"

"Time check," Buffy advised.

Xander did. He was wearing a cheap wristwatch he had purchased at a hamburger joint. It was your regular yellow smiley-faced watch, only this one had three eyes. "Hey! It was only eight! Where was I? Oh no, I wasn't a girl again, was I?"

"'Fraid so," said Buffy. "We were about to give you a makeover."

"Your identity crisis will have to wait," said Giles with a cough. Then, nodding toward MacGovern: "We've more pressing problems."

Xander finally noticed the reporter standing there. "Ah, I don't think we're talking to MacGovern anymore."

The girls automatically took a few steps back from MacGovern. Giles cringed momentarily. Xander sneezed.

Holding his flash camera like a weapon, MacGovern breathed heavily and glared at each of the foursome in turn. A noticeable change had come in his posture. He stood straighter, with his shoulders held high. With a shrug he tried to make his jacket appear a better fit—a hopeless effort. He looked down imperiously at them, easy enough to do from the upper level.

"I know you!" exclaimed Buffy. "You're Cotton Mather. Where's your blood?"

MacGovern/Mather scowled. "I do not know your meaning, sinful one."

"The blood that's supposed to be on your hands!"

He chuckled. "Oh, very good." He inspected the reporter's hands, which at the moment were his own. He appeared to enjoy it. "It is there. These hands are not nearly as clean as MacGovern might wish."

"So Mather's your name, eh?" Xander asked. "What's your—?"

MacGovern silenced him with a gesture. "Don't. You have no idea how many times I heard that phrase in purgatory, where the imagination runs the gamut from A to B."

Buffy was unimpressed. "Still a good question."

MacGovern/Mather smiled, like an angel. "I have returned so I may do my bit, however modest, in unleashing the underworld onto the Earth. It's time for what's currently called a hostile takeover."

"Come on," said Xander, "what's the race of mankind ever done to you?"

"Exist."

"So you're a little bitter," said Willow, trying to be helpful, "and you've had a bad experience these last three-hundred-plus years. But that's no reason to have such a negative approach right now."

Mather drew himself to his full height and pointed his finger straight toward her nose. "Silence, woman! I am not an open book for you to read."

"Doesn't matter," said Buffy quietly. "We already know how you're going to end."

"And you too, unfortunately," snapped back Mather. "Well, I must retrieve an important ingredient for the upcoming resurrection. Bye!" He gathered his arms before him and dove toward a closed window, intending to smash right through it. He stopped at the last possible second, startled practically out of his wits.

"The bars are made of metal in these newer buildings," Giles pointed out. He couldn't resist a smile, even in his condition.

"Curses!" Mather exclaimed, and before they could guess his intentions, he leapt over the railing and landed on the table, square in the middle of the pentagram, knocking down two of the candles. Lightning flashed, followed by deafening thunder, and all the lights in the library cut out for several moments, enough time for lightning to flash yet again. Buffy spent the time stamping out the two flames.

Thus giving Mather the time to jump down and dash out the front door.

"Next time we have a séance, Giles," said Buffy, "you should remember to lock the front door from the inside."

"Point taken," said Giles, just before throwing up.

CHAPTER 8

The black raincoat she'd borrowed from Giles was much too big for Buffy, but at least it had a hood and protected her somewhat from the continuous rain. Though she was on the verge of becoming totally out of breath, she continued running toward the gallery, where she hoped to prevent MacGovern/Mather from obtaining V.V. Vivaldi's Moonman statue.

She ran through an open shopping center, across a small park and through a ritzy neighborhood. Normally when she had this great a distance to make across Sunnydale, she broke down and asked Giles for a lift, but right now he was running a temperature of a hundred and four and was taking a cold shower in the boy's locker room. Xander's job was to take care of Giles, while Willow was surfing the Net hoping to find some kernel of information about Prince Eisenberg, *The Eibon,* V.V. Vivaldi, or anything else that might prevent tonight's events from becoming an absolute rerun of the past.

Buffy hated prophecies. Especially this one. Normally she didn't like to admit to herself that she needed help—even when she knew she did—but she had no problem making an exception in this case. It was too bad Angel wasn't around. He often showed up whenever he was afraid she would get in over her head, but tonight he was nowhere to be seen. She supposed even a conscience-ridden vampire had a social life; that is, if he wasn't out raiding a blood bank somewhere.

At least the raincoat was doing its job. Without her boots, though, her shoes were soaked, and her feet felt wrinkled to a wormlike state by the wet.

Her Slayer instincts were doing their job, too. She knew the Hummer following her belonged to the Churches. They were good at their work too. Every time she took a shortcut or deliberately went down a narrow alley impossible for them to get their jeep through, they always picked her up a short distance down the line.

Buffy had the distinct suspicion the Churches might be more heavily involved in this affair than they'd intended. She also wondered if they were aware of the other set of headlights—belonging to a van—following them. Probably. They were undoubtedly used to occasional media attention by now.

Even so, if she couldn't prevent the Moonman from being stolen, then her task was to keep the four former worshippers of the Despised One from doing a reprise of their "unsavory" dance. She figured that if she could prevent one major element of the original incident from fitting into its proper place, then the entire prophecy might wash away with the smog and pollen in the storm.

Buffy was just a half-mile from the gallery when she finally spotted MacGovern/Mather. He was drenched. He shambled down the center of the street, which tonight was devoid of traffic thanks to the terrific storm; everybody with a semblance of common sense—or no bodily repossessions—was staying home.

She was glad to be able to slow down. Her heart was beating so hard that she was surprised he couldn't hear it, even over the frequent thunder. Still, she edged closer to him, and they were both approximately a hundred yards away from the gallery when Buffy spotted her mother's car parked outside. Naturally. As if it wasn't bad enough she was willfully participating in a scenario that may have killed her in a past life, her mom might discover her daughter is secretly a key player in the eternal struggle between good and evil. *Can you be grounded for eternal life?*

There was only one thing to do, and that was take the bull by the horns and face the situation.

"Mather!" she called out.

MacGovern/Mather stopped and turned. He had been carrying his flash camera the entire time and it was as drenched as he. Rivulets flowed from the brim of his hat and his cheap coat clung to his cheap shirt like plastic wrap. "What do you want? Do not think of interfering," he added, answering his own question.

"Why? Afraid I'll die before my time?" said Buffy, trying to maneuver close enough for an effective attack.

"Doesn't matter when you die, so long as you do. In fact, should you die before the ceremony, so much the better. Reduces the chance of a complication."

"Hmm. It's nice to know you're afraid of complications."

Mather growled and hurled the flash camera at Buffy. She dodged it with ease and it shattered on the sidewalk, exposing the film. It appeared MacGovern's luck would be consistent, in the short-term at least. Buffy couldn't help but laugh.

Mather's reaction was unexpected. Mainly because it was MacGovern's reaction. "Hey, what's so funny?" he asked indignantly. His imperious posture momentarily deflated, only to resume its unnatural height as he said aloud, "Leave me alone. Stay suppressed like you're supposed to, and you might live through this night. You on the other hand"—now he looked at Buffy—"haven't got a prayer."

"Other hand? Sounds to me like you're having trouble keeping the *upper* hand."

Mather, again firmly in control, looked around at the sleek, modern buildings, then glared directly at Buffy. "We knew how to handle smart-mouthed young vixens in my day."

"Burned them at the stake?"

"We were kinder, gentler executioners; we merely hanged them. The barbarians in Europe, they burned the witches!"

"I knew that. I just wanted to hear you deny it." She bent at the knees, bringing forward a branch the size of her arm she'd picked up in the park.

Mather stepped back. Way back. "I deny anything if it's a lie." Lightning flashed behind him, and his shadow cut across the road.

A few blocks down, a Hummer came to a stop and turned out its lights. Then it came forward.

"Deny *this!*" said Buffy. Taking advantage of the distraction, she broke the branch in half—into two pointed stakes—and rolled straight at him, shooting with the force of a bowling ball. Her legs got a little tangled in the raincoat, but otherwise the maneuver went all right.

Mather laughed. She sprang at him, cocking her right arm to drive the stake into his heart.

Or where a heart should be.

Mather dodged the stake with ease. "I once possessed a martial arts master," he explained, while he kicked her in the stomach.

Buffy managed to deflect most of the blow, but it

still delivered quite an impact. She landed on her back, in a manhole up to its rim with water. She rolled out of the way a second before Mather landed on top of her feet-first. She hit him with the bottom of her foot, at the kneecap. His leg crumbled out from under him, and she kicked him in the face.

He grabbed her leg, twisted it—thus twisting her—and sent her flying headfirst into the door of a parked Honda. Luckily the door bent easily.

But she was in the process of standing before she even touched the ground. She turned and threw an underhand stake toward his eye.

He avoided it, knocking it straight down to the ground, but he fell down, which definitely hadn't been part of his plan. He grabbed the stake and threw it back at her.

She caught it.

"Slay me and you slay MacGovern," Mather said. "Possession isn't permanent. Sooner or later I'll have to return control to MacGovern."

Buffy raised her eyebrows. MacGovern/Mather was right. She would have to be more careful.

"How do I know you're not lying?" she asked.

"Maybe my journalist-half is talking!" He turned and ran directly toward the gallery.

Buffy could have caught up with him easily—possessed though he might be, he still had the legs of an old man—but she was momentarily stymied. How should she proceed?

Her mind was made up when Mather, trying to

avoid a huge puddle, brazenly climbed over the hood of Joyce Summers's parked car.

Buffy dashed toward him with murderous intent, but she came to an abrupt stop and slipped and fell onto another car the moment she saw her mother coming out of the gallery.

Mom wasn't alone. With her was the cleaning lady, Pat, who held a bucket filled with cleaning tools in one hand, and with her other hand balanced a mop over her shoulder. Pat was about four-and-a-half-feet tall and weighed nearly 150 pounds; she resembled a fire hydrant.

"Why, Mrs. Summers, how good it is to make your acquaintance," said Mather with a definitely smarmy air. He offered to shake her hand.

"Mister, are you all right?" Buffy's mom asked, peering out from under her umbrella. "You look a fright!"

Buffy watched what happened next in a car mirror. The moment Mather made a false move, the stakes would start to fly!

"Look a fright?" exclaimed Mather. "I am a fright!"

He grabbed Mrs. Summers by the wrist and yanked her toward him. She spun into his arms and he held her in a bear hug. It had taken only a second.

But it was long enough for Buffy to expose herself and cock back her right arm. She had her eye on the nape of his neck.

Joyce had hers on his foot. She stamped it with the point of her high heel.

Mather yelled and released her, thus giving Pat the cleaning lady a clear shot with her mop. She caught Mather upside the head and he staggered away from them, toward the stairs leading to the gallery.

"The gallery is closed, sir," said Joyce Summers, who had already gotten her cell phone from her pocketbook and was dialing 911.

"That depends on your perspective," Mather replied. He had steadied himself by the time he'd reached the top of the stairs, and when he turned toward the front door he broke out into a full run, giving the others the distinct impression he would try to run straight through it. Instead, he veered at the last possible instant and ran straight into a window. No iron bars! Glass and wood shattered, as he disappeared into the gallery. A slew of alarms went off, but Mather obviously didn't care.

No respect for the human body whatsoever, thought Buffy, moving down the line of parked cars. She had to follow Mather, regardless of whether or not her mother spotted her. *Besides, if I live through tonight I can be grounded forever, for all I care. In fact, I could use the rest.* But it would be better if her mother didn't see her. She pulled the hood closer.

"Shouldn't we go after him?" asked Pat, raising her voice to be heard.

"No, leave the heroics to the professionals," Joyce replied. "Hello? 911? I'd like to report a break-in."

Thanks, Mom, thought Buffy as she took advantage of the moment, the darkness and all the alarms and dashed across the sidewalk with the fleetness of a cat in hunting mode. She realized her dilemma had gotten worse, if that was possible. Now she was faced with the choice of either stopping Mather before the police came or letting him be arrested for attempting to steal the Vivaldi Moonman. Either way, Darryl MacGovern, streetwise but unlucky reporter, would take the rap.

Buffy found the upraised path along the side of the gallery so narrow she had no choice but to walk directly under the rain that rolled off the rooftop like a waterfall. It was like getting hit in the head with a succession of buckets of water. But at least it enabled her to see inside.

Most businesses leave at least half the lights on after closing to discourage unwelcome visitors. The gallery was no exception. Buffy saw through a window, and through an open door beyond, into a room where a drenched Mather was examining the podium upon which stood the Moonman statue. Naturally it looked just like the statue on Buffy's dream notebook. Like a standing jigsaw puzzle of a man with a broken face.

Buffy broke the window with her elbow, reached inside and opened it. Normally she wasn't so up front about breaking and entering, but she figured tonight she could make an exception because the alarms already made it sound like the whole city had been struck by a giant earthquake.

But by the time she reached the podium, Mather had already knocked it over and taken the statue. She looked down the hall just in time to see him closing the back door behind him.

Then she looked up the hall just in time to see the first policeman coming in.

He had a flashlight. She could almost feel the beam hitting the back of her head as she pulled up her hood and ran toward the back door. He called out for her to stop.

He fired one shot into the air—at least she hoped it was in the air—so she zoomed from the gallery rear exit with an extra burst of speed. Mather was nowhere to be seen, which was a problem, but she had to make sure the same thing could be said about her before the policeman's backup arrived.

Near the fence in the rear were two bushes just far enough apart to provide her with cover for a few moments while she thought of her next move. She dove in.

And landed right on top of Mather. They bumped heads so hard she saw stars.

By the time Buffy recovered enough to think straight, Mather was already gone—he'd probably climbed over the fence—and the rear of the gallery was now crawling with police.

Actually, there were only two who were inspecting the grounds—two too many under the circumstances. Buffy had no choice but to lay low, hugging the mud while the rain poured down. Her only consolation was that she was behind enough cover so the cops couldn't see her when the lightning flashed.

By the time the police were gone and it was safe for Buffy to climb over the rear fence, Mather was nowhere to be seen. Any trail he might have left behind was by now washed away. To make matters worse, neither the Hummer nor the van were visible. One would have thought that Eric Frank's face would be everywhere, looking for angles on the theft of the infamous Moonman statue.

Buffy refused to give up, however, and she trotted down the street looking for a sign.

CHAPTER 9

But first, a phone call. When she found a phone booth, Buffy discovered she had no change, so she had to call the library collect. She just hoped Giles was still conscious enough to accept the charges.

Buffy's heart sank when Willow answered. At least she accepted the call.

"Giles is so hot he's practically steaming," Willow said. "But he's not getting any worse. According to the slayer histories, Robert Erwin didn't die until a few days after Sarah Dinsdale's escape, so we think Giles will be okay until . . . after . . . well, you know. . . ."

"Believe me. You haven't mentioned Xander."

"That's because he went looking for you."

"I thought he was supposed to—"

"Buffy, he's as much tied up in this as you are. No one wants you to face this alone."

"Yes, but I'm hoping to keep Xander and myself separated, to change the equation so to speak."

"Oh. I take it he hasn't found you yet."

"Well, if he went to the gallery, he might have been distracted by all the police running about. Have you found anything yet?"

"No. I've been racking my brains, but I have no idea where a ceremony with a false Stonehenge setting can take place in the Sunnydale area. At the moment I'm stuck in a chatroom with some British witches who claimed to have erected the original Stonehenge in a previous life. They're a little confused, though, on which of the three major building periods they were involved with—"

"And the weather?"

"All the weather sites are confused. There was no indication anywhere in the atmosphere that the Pacific Coast was going to be hit by a storm this large and fierce. Flash-flood warnings are in effect from Seattle to San Diego."

"Get me some cold medicine. I'll be back eventually." Buffy sneezed. "See you."

"Ciao," Willow said weakly, and then they both hung up.

Buffy figured she might as well stay in the phone booth while she tried to think of what to do next. She was tired and cold and worried, and she was barely able to hold in check her anxieties about her role in the prophecy. Were Slayers supposed to die until one of them finally got it right, or did they always die? Perhaps the best thing for her and Xander to do would be to screw things up completely by leaving town, where they couldn't possibly be affected or drawn in.

But then again, maybe things would be even worse if they did. That was the trouble with fate. You never knew when you had reached another fork in the road.

The phone booth was on the perimeter of a parking lot of a convenience store that recently went out of business. Next to the phone booth was the only shining lamppost for two hundred yards. On the other side of the street were two empty lots that despite being prime land had gone unused for Sunnydale's entire history. The rain showed no sign of easing up.

Buffy thought seriously about giving up and just going back to the library. She didn't even know where to head first.

A car passed, splashing up so much water that a huge wave struck the side of the phone booth. Unfortunately, this phone booth was open at the bottom. Until that moment, Buffy's knees had been dry.

She made up her mind and strode out of the booth. She didn't put up her hood; there was no point. She was halfway across the road when she came to a dead stop.

For a few seconds she had no idea why. Her

survival instincts occasionally compelled her to do things without knowing why. Usually in retrospect her senses had picked up on something her conscious mind hadn't noticed. Such as the moving mound in the mud in one of the empty lots.

Another car approached, forcing Buffy to finish crossing the street. She veered in the direction of the mound. She twirled the stake in her right hand. No doubt about it—something underground was approaching her. It couldn't be good.

Whatever senses it possessed, however, were severely limited. It went right under the sidewalk and disappeared for several moments. She imagined it—a giant, carnivorous worm? a deadly multi-bladed machine?—hitting the underside of the asphalt several times in an effort to break through and restore whatever dim bead it had on her.

The mound revealed itself again. It moved away from the sidewalk in a different direction; the two lines in the dirt formed a "V."

Buffy hurled a stake at the moving mound. The stake spun like an axis, glistening in a lightning flash, and stuck straight up in the dirt. It quivered for a few moments, then rose straight up in the air. At least that's what it looked like.

Until the zombie's head rose out of the ground, quickly followed by the rest of its body. At that moment Buffy would have gladly traded all the stakes in creation for one good minute with a surface-to-air missile launcher.

The zombie turned to face her. Its own face was pretty rank: most of the skin had been scraped off underground. It wore buckskins and its putrefying hair was tied in ponytails; once it had been a warrior. When it growled, a strip of rotten skin fluttered where its Adam's apple should have been.

Once the warrior had lost an arm at the elbow. With that lost arm he'd held a hatchet. The zombie held that same arm, which was holding that same hatchet, right now.

It advanced.

Buffy sighed. That missile launcher sure would have saved a lot of time. As it was now, dispatching this zombie would take a few minutes longer.

So she became the missile, launching herself at it feet first. She was betting that it couldn't move very fast without accelerating its decay, and she was about half-right.

It grabbed her feet with its remaining hand, but it had to drop the forearm with the hatchet to do so.

It still couldn't stop her, really. She buried both her feet into its chest up to her ankles. Bone cracked big-time and Buffy winced; the experience was like jumping from a diving board onto a giant snail.

They both went down in a heap, with Buffy on top. The zombie fell badly, breaking apart under the combined impact of Buffy and the sidewalk. Buffy fell almost as badly, hurting the small of her back. But that didn't stop her from rolling away from the pieces of the zombie as quickly as possible.

A putrefied hand clung to her raincoat. Buffy broke its fingers in half one by one, and then stamped her foot on the hand until it was mush. The fingers still crawled toward her like worms. The rest of the zombie was attempting the same. A shoulder scooted, the head rolled and the one standing leg hopped. Their intentions did not look good.

Buffy knew she couldn't just leave them because that head was bound to bite somebody before it got itself kicked in, but as she waited for a car—and its startled driver!—to pass by, she got the distinct impression somebody else was growling at her.

She turned to face a fieldful of zombies rising from the earth.

They seemed to have no leader and no mind, group or otherwise. They simply shambled toward her, apparently with no other intention than just killing her.

This was bad, more than just a tough jam. Buffy remembered the dream of Samantha Kane being menaced by parts of a zombie, not to mention Sarah Dinsdale's story of what happened to the men trying to recapture her. They had been set upon by a horde of zombies. *Like a gaggle of geese,* Buffy thought grimly.

She got ready, stooping to a fighting stance. It might take a while, but she was sure she could eradicate them, with or without the stake she'd dropped. She changed her mind when four zombies scooped up the parts of their fallen comrade along the way and ate them. (The one without a lower jaw stuffed pieces of the foot, including a shoe, down his throat.) She had decided to look for the nearest bulldozer or any other piece of equipment that would help her mash these things as flat as possible, as quickly as possible.

Seeing nothing of potential help in the immediate vicinity, she took off into the alley between the empty store and a deserted office building and climbed over a wire-mesh fence into a dark, wet grade school lot and ran as fast as she could.

On the other side of the lot she slowed down and saw the zombies still following her, though they had no hope of maintaining her pace, much less overtaking her.

Buffy waited until most of them were halfway across the lot, then she climbed over the fence and landed on the sidewalk. Across the street lay Sunnydale Central Park.

She had an idea. It was risky and broke every Slayer rule in the book, but that had never stopped her before. So that there would be absolutely no chance they'd lose sight of her, she sauntered into the park as if on a Sunday stroll. Now she was entering well-lit territory. The sidewalks and open spaces were so bright the rain glistened like sunlight on the sea, and even the tops of the pines were lit. Luckily the weather was so bad even the delinquents who usually hung out there had gone home.

Buffy turned around (though she kept walking backward) and saw the zombies shuffling across the street. Tires screeched and a car crashed into something nearby. Buffy tensed. All the zombies she saw were still coming toward her, but she had no idea if she was drawing them *all* away or—

Someone screamed. Gunshots were fired. There was a second car crash.

No, some zombies had definitely become distracted. *Curses!* Now she had to double back to make sure no one was being eaten.

She began to make an arc, but when she reached a pedestrian lane at the edge of the park leading back across the street, she stopped and let out a little cry of frustration.

And no wonder. Coming straight toward her was another zombie army, though this one was dressed more like the Spaniards from the early days of California history, complete with metal helmets and chest plates. Obviously they were going to be more difficult to stomp to death than the army of zombies already chasing her. It appeared checking up on whoever was in the automobiles would have to wait, perhaps indefinitely.

Currently on the same wavelength, the two sets of zombies simply flowed into one great stream; they still followed her just as relentlessly, just as mindlessly. They weren't even fazed when one was struck by a bolt of lightning and turned into cinder.

Buffy kept about a hundred yards between herself and the zombies. She stayed in sight. She tried not to put too many barriers between herself and the shambling creatures because she wasn't sure they possessed the smarts to navigate past them. When she ran through a tennis court she was sure she'd been right: some zombies went through the openings, but others tried climbing the wire-mesh fence rather than going around it. Most succeeded, incidentally, but a few fell all the way down and broke apart upon hitting the ground. The ones that still had legs and torso attached gathered themselves together as best as they could and straggled behind.

Three-quarters of the way through the park Buffy sighted the town gazebo in the middle of an open stretch of ground. According to legend, a brass band had played under the gazebo every Sunday until the advent of the Jazz Age, and the people of Sunnydale gathered on the grounds to listen and do all the other things people of small towns were supposed to have done during the glorious "Past."

The notion of resting and getting out of the rain for five minutes was appealing. Indeed, with the way the zombies were advancing toward her, maybe she could take a catnap.

She was just bounding the stairs, however, when she realized that all of a sudden she wasn't alone.

Of course, neither were the startled Cordelia and the second-string halfback she was making out with, the snotty Augie Duluth. "Buffy!" exclaimed

Cordelia, as she broke away from Augie and tried to hide how disheveled her hair and clothing were. "Invade personal space much?"

"Getting out of the rain?"

"You can't! I'm busy!" Cordelia replied, as an undeterred Augie pursed his lips, grabbed her, spun her back to him, and attempted to suck face with all the finesse girls usually expect from members of the football team.

Buffy's stomach turned: she didn't find Augie attractive in the slightest. Then, with a rear glance, she remembered why she'd come here in the first place. The zombies were nowhere to be seen—not yet—but their distinct growl was faintly audible, if one knew what to listen for. "Cordelia, I think it's time you blew this gazebo!"

"I beg your pardon?" Cordelia exclaimed.

"All right! My little dew flower!" Augie exclaimed, just before he planted yet another big wet sloppy kiss on her.

Somebody better throw this dog a Milkbone, thought Buffy. "The police are coming!"

Cordelia jumped away from Augie as if he'd given her an electric shock. "What?"

"I'm sorry," said Buffy sheepishly, "but I've gotten into trouble with the law. They're on their way," she added, pointing to the trees.

"Why should I go?" Cordelia asked. "I didn't do anything wrong."

"Just think of the social black eye you'll get if the

word leaks that you were hanging with a known felon."

"Don't tell me you burnt down the *Sunnydale* gym too," said Augie with a laugh.

"Only the boys' locker room," said Buffy. "All those smelly gym socks needed was one spark and . . . *poof!*"

"You said you're in trouble with whom?" Cordelia asked. At last the full implication of what Buffy was saying had sunk in and she was genuinely shocked.

Buffy saw the first pair of zombie legs become visible beneath the distant foliage. "You'll read about it in the papers tomorrow. Just trust me and go!"

"She's right, babe," said Augie. "See you around, my little jailbird," he said to Buffy as he took Cordelia by the elbow and attempted to escort her down the steps.

But Cordelia was reluctant and she glared at Buffy. "You're involved in more funny business, aren't you?"

"You don't want to know."

Suddenly energized, Cordelia slapped a surprised Augie several times on the arm. "What's keeping you? Let's go!" She grabbed him by his varsity jacket and practically dragged him into the rain. "You're so slow!"

"That's not—"

"Shut up!" Cordelia hissed.

Buffy sighed with relief that they were finally going. She hated to admit it, but at the moment she envied Cordelia, who for all her faults was at least living a normal teenager's life.

And then of course there were the zombies, who had already lived theirs. The army shuffled down the hill toward the gazebo. A few slipped and fell, knocking others over and breaking off more than a few limbs in the process. Their chorus of growls was not inspired by the self-inflicted carnage or by the carnage they hoped to inflict on Buffy—they just came out spontaneously.

"Oh Romeo, oh Romeo, about time you showed up." Buffy had no idea if any of the zombies had enough brains left to be taunted, but she'd noticed a couple of them veering off in the direction Cordelia and Augie had taken. She needed them all to follow her, without exception, if her plan was to work.

The zombies did. Buffy leapt off the gazebo, landed on the first stone of a raised path and headed out the park past a baseball field and a deserted public building. Well, at least she hoped it was deserted. It certainly appeared closed for the night, which was good, because in a few minutes she wouldn't be able to deal with any strays.

She crossed the street by now so drenched that she thought nothing of fording the water overflowing the gutters on either side.

Buffy reached the border of a well-groomed field that was off-limits to the public. Beyond the field was a well-lit building surrounded by an electrified fence covered with barbed wire. During the few seconds Buffy glanced that way, the building's lightning rod attracted no less than three bolts.

Then, without trying to be too circumspect about it, she ducked into an underground tunnel. It was a two-way road, with each lane just large enough to handle a Mack truck. The parking lot it served was over two hundred yards away, below the other side of the well-groomed field. There were no doors, no emergency exits. The only way in or out was at either side.

Buffy hesitated, thought of something, then dashed back out into the street. Sure enough, the zombies showed every sign of missing her, of wandering by. She put two fingers to her lips and whistled loudly. She waved. "Hey! Adoring masses! This way!"

She went back into the tunnel, pausing until she saw that the zombies were following her this time. Then she ran. The zombie's growls echoed eerily throughout the tunnel; they rang in her ears like curses. The farther she went into the tunnel, the narrower and darker it seemed. It was all Buffy could do to refrain from running full-tilt to put as much distance between her and the zombies as possible. When she saw the guard in the booth up ahead, she knew she had to slow down.

Slow down and try to think of a way to save him.

Perhaps the best approach, she thought, would be an honest one. "Hey, mister!" she called out.

Uh-oh! The "mister" was a woman. A *police-woman*. She got out of the booth, where she'd been reading a paperback novel. On one side of her belt hung a nightstick, while on the other hung a holster heavy with the biggest sidearm Buffy had ever seen. The officer was in the process of pulling her gun from its holster when she saw that she had been startled by a teenager.

"Girl!" exclaimed the officer. "What are you doing out on a night like this?"

"I'm being followed. May I borrow that?" Without waiting for an answer, she freed the nightstick from the officer's holster.

"Hey!" she cried at Buffy.

"Relax," said Buffy, pointing the nightstick down the tunnel. "I just need to make a point."

The zombies shuffled into view, their zombie-ness further distorted by the parking lot's lights. The policewoman gasped in disbelief. Buffy got the balance of the nightstick and then threw it briskly, just like a butterknife, at the foremost zombie.

The stick went through its forehead like a hot blowtorch through a gallon of ice cream.

Still the zombie approached. The fact that most of its brains had been pushed out of its ears had no effect whatsoever on its overall performance.

The officer screamed, and Buffy didn't blame her; most people went about their daily business unprepared for confrontations with formerly dead people dropping body parts. "Better run," Buffy suggested. "I'll be right behind you."

They backed up into a heavily fenced parking lot.

Buffy quickly scoped out the situation. She stood at the border of the lot where the police and guards kept their civilian vehicles. Buffy knew the place would soon be swarming with cops, thanks to the officer's continuous screaming.

Buffy smiled to herself. *Life could be good, after all.*

She turned to the approaching zombies—the one with the big hole in its forehead now brandished the nightstick awkwardly, but no less threateningly—and whistled at them again. "Hi, boys, new in town?" she called out. "My name's Buffy and I know how to show you a real good time."

The zombie with the hole in its forehead still had two good dead eyes. It growled so deeply parts of its neck fluttered out and hit the blacktop with a sickening *plop!*. Another zombie nearby scooped up the debris and stuffed it into its mouth, swallowing several of its own teeth in the process. Even though all the zombies weren't out of the tunnel yet, their leaders—that is, the ones who happened to be at the front or close to it—advanced toward Buffy.

Buffy backed up some more. The idea was to lure the zombies as far as possible into the parking lot, an idea which, now that she thought about, was working better and faster than she'd ever anticipated. All the zombies were now inside, and she had no choice but to slow down, because the zombies were trying to maneuver her back against the wall.

Buffy tried to circle around using a couple of parked automobiles for interference, but while they couldn't exactly taste flesh and blood, the zombies were becoming excited, in their own detached way, about the prospect of soon feasting on the meal that had thus far eluded them.

Buffy slammed back against a van. Zombies approached to the front of her. To the right of her. To the left. She looked down to see a blackened hand reaching out from beneath the van, groping for her. She ground her heel on the hand with all the might she could muster, turned, jumped, grabbed the luggage rack and swung onto the top of the van.

A zombie was already crawling up to greet her. She kicked it under the skin. The head lifted completely from the torso with a *rip* that echoed throughout the underground lot. She turned and kicked another zombie in the chest.

Oops! My fault!

This time when her foot went into a zombie's chest, this one helped keep it there by grabbing her ankle with both hands and twisting it. Buffy had to twist her entire body to keep her leg from being broken. Her greatest fear at the moment was that she would fall off the van, but she managed to stay on the top, landing face-first with her outstretched palms absorbing most of the impact. She drew in both her knees, then kicked with both feet, sending the zombie flying into three zombies scrambling over one another in their efforts to get to the top.

The four zombies fell in a heap. At that moment Officer McCrumski entered the area ready for the night shift. He saw a young woman clinging to the top of his partner's minivan. "Hey, what are you. . . ." He trailed off, his breakfast sandwich falling to the pavement. He fumbled for his gun.

The zombies didn't care. Those who weren't climbing up the van simply turned toward the thin blue line.

Uh-oh! Buffy rolled off the van, on the opposite side of the policeman, the moment he began firing. This gave her protection from the bullets but not from the zombies who happened to be on the other side. They caught her before she hit the ground and immediately tried to pull her apart or eat her, whichever was easiest.

Wonder if Prince Ashton predicted this, Buffy thought sardonically, as she kicked off the face of a zombie trying to bite her ankle. She twisted and jabbed her elbow into another one. It got stuck between the creature's ribs. She hooked her elbow in deeper and then yanked with all her might; her fist struck another zombie on the sternum with such force that it pressed against the spine and all the organs in between squished out the other side.

Only to be caught and eaten by other zombies.

Buffy and the zombies holding her fell down in a heap. She fought herself free and grabbed a headless, legless torso and tried to use it as a shield against the other zombies. That part of the idea was good, but the fact that the arms were still attached and quite active made for a bad complication. The arms reached backward and tried to pull her hair out. Buffy wound up bumping the torso against attacking zombies as she tried to pull off the arms and hide behind the car parked next to the van.

Meanwhile, the zombies advancing on Officer McCrumski were literally cut into pieces by the bullets. One dropped a shoulder. One chest was hit hard enough that it split in half, right down the middle.

McCrumski emptied his revolver without thinking. Now he held a smoking gun against an invasion of . . . *mutants,* he thought. *Probably rejects from a drug research program.*

He took another look at the advancing perps, threw his empty gun at them and bolted for the stationhouse.

Buffy half-crawled, half-ran behind the line of parked cars, heading for the nearby access road to Route 13. She needed to lead them away from the station before anybody got a good look at them. Once she did that, she had to disappear herself. Without a quarry they should return to the cemetery. *Brain-dead lemmings,* she thought.

The manhole ahead presented some interesting possibilities.

With what felt like the last of her strength she whirled and threw the torso she'd been using for protection at a zombie who'd so far managed to gain on her. The zombie caught the torso and began nibbling at what was left of the neck. Meanwhile, Buffy summoned just enough energy to lift the manhole cover and push it away.

She crawled into pitch darkness, into the sewer. She closed the cover behind her.

The sewer tunnel was tall enough to permit her to stand as she walked. Since she couldn't see anything, she simply picked a direction.

After a while her gag reflex kicked in to such a degree that she was afraid she would vomit everything she'd eaten since the age of six. Her only consolation was a sliver of light in the distance, an indication, perhaps, of another manhole leading out of this tunnel.

She hoped it was still raining. Right now she smelled worse than all those zombies put together, and getting drenched yet again would be a blessing.

CHAPTER 10

It was your average manhole cover. It filled in the hole leading to the sewer, and didn't collapse whenever a car, truck or what-have-you ran over it. At the moment it lay there in the rain, doing its job, while not far away a steady barrage of gunfire testified to the ferocity of the zombie attack on the police force.

A couple of fingers, whose nails desperately needed to be redone, poked through the holes in the manhole cover. They slipped back down the moment before they were run over by a passing automobile.

A few more moments passed, then the fingers poked through again, more gingerly this time. They pressed down, hard.

The manhole cover moved with a sudden jerk. It lay in the middle of the street while Buffy Summers stuck her head through the hole and made sure no more traffic was coming. Then she crawled out on her hands and knees and, with a weakness she found frightening, pushed the manhole cover back into place.

It lay there, once again doing its job, while Buffy dashed to the sidewalk and tried to ignore the fact that right now *she* was the only source of the incredible stench causing her to gag. She fell onto her knees, tried to catch her breath, and spent a few luxurious moments feeling the rain wash away the grease and grime from her clothing.

Well, she hoped no one at the police station had gotten hurt—no one who was still alive, anyway. And while it might have been bad–heroine form to desert the police, she really hadn't been in much of a position to help. Her main concern was her mom and the prophecy. In that order.

Checking her pockets, she realized with despair that she'd lost every dollar bill she had (five, to be exact) in the sewer, if not before. Buffy rarely carried her pocketbook while on the hunt, but a certain amount of money was a necessity.

Then, relieved, she found one soggy dollar in her hip pocket. It was pressed flat; it must have gone through the washer/drier a couple of times. Buffy was afraid to unwrap it, but she clutched it like the life-saver it was. Time to phone home again.

Buffy had done a bunch of slaying at a nearby post office. It kept the doors to its lobby open twenty-four hours so innocent victims could get bitten by vampires and become part of the legions of the undead any time at night, all because they wanted some stamps. She headed there in the hope one of the change machines would break her soggy dollar.

Having had enough of short cuts and underpopulated parts of Sunnydale for the evening, she stuck to the main road. The post office was about a mile away on the other side of the interstate. She could make it in less than ten minutes if she trotted at a not-too-arduous pace.

But she never made it as far as the interstate, much less to the post office. Next to the underpass was a popular truck stop called Billy Bob's Steak House, famous for having, as its slogan said, "the fastest food in the West." *But hardly ever in the way Billy Bob intended,* Xander was fond of saying.

Even so, in the storm the Steak House's neon lights promised both change and temporary shelter. She wondered how much they charged for a cup of coffee.

Buffy had never eaten there—it didn't exactly cater to the social ambitions of high school students—but judging from how packed the parking lot was, the food must be popular with people passing through town. Especially truckers—for several semis, some with their engines still running so the drivers wouldn't have to waste time warming them up, sat in the largest wing of the parking lot.

Another wing was filled with approximately forty less specialized vehicles, plus about ten motorcycles belonging to members of a local club. Buffy slowed, forgetting for the moment she was in the middle of a thunderstorm, when she noticed a familiar Hummer. The Churches' Hummer.

Parked right beside it was the van with the raining frogs logo painted on the side. The Churches and the crew of *Charles Fort's Peculiar World* were evidently having a bite to eat here.

Buffy scowled. Could it be that Cotton Mather, in the body of Darryl MacGovern, and with a certain purloined statue fashioned from moonrock in tow, was sampling modern cuisine in the company of Judge Danforth, Sheriff Corwin and Heather Putnam?

That dollar was more important than ever now. Buffy had to contact Willow at the library and find out if she could confirm that the showdown was fated to happen here, at a country steak house.

She sneezed. Suddenly Buffy saw her own future, all by herself: she was going to spend the next three or four days in bed, nursing a cold of Olympian proportions. If she lived through tonight, that is.

She looked through the Hummer's windows. She saw an unfolded map of Stonehenge in the back seat, lying right next to one of the gallery's notebooks with a picture of V.V. Vivaldi's Moonman statue on the cover.

Buffy moved to the van and looked through the rear window, where she saw something definitely exceptional: the cameraman and the soundman sitting in the back trussed up like turkeys, gagged, blindfolded and lying amid their scattered equipment. It was easy to see what had happened, even if they, as Buffy suspected, did not. Possessed by one of the loose spirits, Eric Frank had overcome them.

And had gone inside. Every sense Buffy had rang like a bell. This was it. Everything was going to happen again. The manipulator of events was going to rise, just as the Despised One had attempted three hundred years ago. Truly a case of a living rerun.

Only people usually know in advance how a rerun turns out, Buffy thought. *But not tonight. Tonight it's going to be him or me, but not both!*

Buffy grimaced. She took off her raincoat, wrapped it around her fist and pulled back, aiming for the window. She knew she had no choice but to start the festivities by freeing the crew.

Or maybe she did have a choice. Sure, she was obligated to free them, but nothing in the prophecy said anything about people standing around taking pictures.

She could free them later.

Good. The less distractions, the better. Looked

like the crowd was up to capacity inside, which amounted to approximately one hundred and fifty other distractions.

Billy Bob's was boomerang-shaped, like an urban bus stop, but with one wing, that of the restaurant itself, vastly lengthened. That wing had three long, wide picture windows providing Buffy with a pretty good view of the layout despite the distance between them. There were booths, all filled, at the windows, a long bar at the rear where the truckers ate and round, wooden tables in between. Part of the kitchen extended into the wing, and the chefs handed the busy waitresses their meals through a large portal.

Neither Frank nor the Churches were in view and neither were, come to think of it, Darryl MacGovern and the Moonman. But not all booths were visible. They undoubtedly sat in one of those.

She couldn't help noticing the portions were huge. Her mouth watered at the odors that not even the storm could wash away. She made a mental note to have lunch at this place after it was rebuilt.

Glancing at the short wing, which comprised a huge filling station and some facilities the truckers could use to tune up their vehicles, Buffy marched for the front doors. She kept a lookout for stray zombies on the way. Those creatures had been as singleminded as it was possible for a dead organism to be.

She slowed down as she stepped under an awning—at last, relief from the rain!—and assumed the demeanor of a distressed girl who'd been caught in the storm. She wrung out her hair, but since she was soaked from head to toe, that hardly made a dent in her overall dampness.

She walked to the swinging doors and was about to push one open when someone on the other side opened it before she did.

"Honey, are you okay?" drawled a waitress with a pile of red hair that reached out to Jupiter. She wore a canary yellow uniform, and had clearly been on her way outside for a cigarette break. "I didn't see you coming."

"That's all right," said Buffy cheerfully, but still acting distressed. "I didn't see you either."

"Honey, what happened to you?" the waitress asked.

"You know. Bicycle. Rain. The Weather Channel."

"That's a shame, honey."

"Is there a place where I can dry off?"

"Better than that, there's a place where we can put you in a waitress uniform while your clothes dry. How's that?"

Buffy grinned. "Perfect."

The waitress's name turned out to be Edith. She took Buffy to a dressing room to the side of the kitchen opposite the serving portal. There the waitresses changed in and out of their "civvies." While the uniforms were perfectly presentable to the general public, they had a certain tackiness that made the waitresses want to wear them in the world beyond Billy Bob's as little as possible.

Buffy understood how they felt the moment she put on one of the uniforms. The big white apron with its cartoonishly large bows on the back made her feel like she was dressed like a doll at a costume party. The fact that the yellow uniform's "small" size was still too large for her made the feeling worse.

And don't even talk to me about the hairnet. Way not!

But at least wearing the uniform might allow her to snoop around without being noticed. Furthermore, she had to make another call. After throwing her clothes in the washing machine with a bunch of clothes that looked as filthy as anything she'd seen in the sewer, she made change with the lady at the cash register and went to the public phones near the front door.

She still couldn't see in all the booths. Whoever was in the booth all the way to the end of the wing was in Edith's territory, and they seemed to be demanding a lot of attention from her. Buffy wondered what she could say to Edith that would make sense *and* would induce her to split this scene as quickly as possible.

Well, she'd think of something. First, she had to "phone home."

"Willow! What do you have for me?"

"Nothing!" came the slightly desperate reply. "What do you have for me?"

"I'm going to treat you to a steak after all this is over!" said Buffy.

"Why? Save it for the vampires." Her voice was distant and distracted on the other end of the line.

"No, no, I mean steak as in Billy Bob's Country Steak House. That's where I am, and I have to tell you, I'm coming back when I have time to eat. Anyway, I think MacGovern and the three missing souls are seriously chowing down here, but I haven't seen them yet. Even so, this is where the prophecy's going to go down. I can feel it. Did you say you haven't found out anything?"

"Yeah sorry, Buffy, but I've been in every techno-pagan chat room I can think of, and no one has any info remotely helpful."

"Figures, there's never a good voodoo priestess around when you need one. How's Giles?"

"Sick as a dog. He's got an icepack on his head and his feet in a bucket of ice, but his temperature is bad. I may have to call an ambulance!"

"Any word from Xander?"

"He hasn't come back. I bet he finds you first."

"Right. I'll check in as soon as the fun's over. Ciao!"

Suddenly someone opened both the swinging front doors smack into her.

I've gotta work on this in-and-out thing, she thought, then stopped cold.

Xander.

But that was just her first impression. A closer look, focusing on his posture, revealed that Sarah had asserted herself and was definitely in control of Xander's body. Unused to walking in the body of a man, "she" stood and walked stiffly, very unlike Xander's normal gait, as if he had become a female mannequin.

Luckily, Xander/Sarah did not recognize Buffy. The seventeenth-century witch might have known her as a participant in the séance, but the waitress outfit was an effective distraction.

But while Xander, to whatever degree he might have been self-aware, was no doubt concerned about Buffy's safety, Sarah clearly had other people on her mind. He/she strode purposefully down the steak house, weaving among the crowded tables.

Xander/Sarah stopped at the furthermost booth. She said something in an agitated manner, gesturing with an air suggesting that it had taken a lot of nerve.

The something must have been shocking, judging from how everyone in the immediate vicinity grew quiet and looked at Xander/Sarah as if he was a crazy person.

Buffy recognized that things were clearly coming to a head. Xander/Sarah backed up; the moment of determination and will had given way to doubt and fear.

Some guy stood and turned, frowning at Xander/Sarah with arms folded across his chest with the contempt only those who are utterly evil can bring to bear. The body belonged to Rick Church, but the stooped shoulders revealed the true personality to be that of elderly Judge Danforth.

"Pray to your betters, Sarah Dinsdale!" Danforth said in a booming voice. "Bow before us. Perhaps you'll give us reason to show mercy."

"Sarah? Who's Sarah?" asked some of the customers aloud to friends or those close by, and most everyone chuckled or giggled as they eyed Xander.

Only Xander/Sarah cowered before this man. The crowd might be amused but she was the only one who knew the truth: This man was about to call up the forces of darkness.

At the moment, Buffy was more afraid of the crowd. So far she'd tried to avoid doing her Slayer stuff before strangers, especially a hundred and fifty of them. This place undoubtedly had security cameras. That meant she'd really be doing her thing before the entirety of civilization as she knew it today.

People forget, Giles had once said. *Cameras remember. Forever.*

Meanwhile, Rick/Danforth became angry at the crowd. He seethed with anger barely contained, his emotions struggling with a strong disbelief factor. After all, he wasn't used to having the common rabble treat him with such disrespectful familiarity.

"You people are doomed," he said. "It awes me to see such ignorant buffoons embrace their destruction so enthusiastically. So be it."

He snapped his fingers. He waited.

Three other people rose out of the booth. On the surface they were Lora Church, Eric Frank and Darryl MacGovern.

Almost. They didn't act like Lora, Eric and Darryl. MacGovern/Mather held forth the Vivaldi Moonman in one hand like a club, just in case Buffy doubted he had possession of it. Lora's posture, meanwhile, had changed from that of a woman to that of an awkward adolescent, like Heather. And Frank's obnoxious demeanor had changed into the stern malevolence of Sheriff Corwin.

And once again they had Sarah in captivity. Her talents would augment and complete their circle of power.

Buffy realized she never would have known this if it hadn't been for the dreams. The patrons had no reason to suspect the four standing were anything other than they appeared to be, two well-dressed yuppies along with two reporters with bad fashion instincts. And a guy named Sarah. The patrons had no idea what they were dealing with.

This is it, Buffy realized. *All the pieces are in place. Our rerun is imminent.*

Rick/Danforth's fingers snapped and produced the tiniest flash of light, so tiny Buffy was certain she was one of the few who caught it.

Buffy realized she couldn't wait any longer. She had to do something.

And then the zombies hit.

CHAPTER 11

The zombies were hard to miss. They came crashing through the front windows. A line of zombies marched double-time through the entrance, while another line came charging from the men's room and a third came from the lady's. They'd evidently come in through the bathroom windows.

The first thing Buffy noticed about this army of the undead was that it was well-armed with the latest in assault weaponry.

Most of the zombies were derived from the corpses of old men, though quite a few had been young men, and a good number of corpses from both categories had been maimed before the ravages of decay had set in.

Buffy remembered there was a Veterans of Foreign Wars cemetery in Sunnydale. They must have hit an armory on the way over.

Needless to say, the crowd's reaction was immediate. People screamed and tried to scramble away, but a few of the zombies fired in the air. Lights burst and debris fell from the ceiling while the people screamed again and dropped to the floor— the way they'd seen innocent bystanders do in movies whenever there was gunfire in a crowded situation.

Only Edith, Buffy and the possessed people were left standing; Xander/Sarah was still cowering.

Edith had realized she was one of the few still standing, and she'd also recognized that Buffy stood her ground like someone who knew how to handle herself whenever she was surrounded by massive armies of the undead. Though *how* she recognized that, Edith wasn't sure. She *was* sure, however, that she'd quit smoking the minute she got out of this alive.

Buffy pointed to the floor. Edith nodded, got down and crawled out of the immediate vicinity while trying to be as inconspicuous as possible.

"What's next, people?" Buffy asked. "Turkey dinner?"

"I do not understand," said Lora/Heather. "Was that supposed to be humorous, child?"

Buffy bristled. She had her hands in fists and she

made tiny steps back and forth, very indecisively. She would have had no problem doing something about the zombies—she might have even charged right in at the possessed people—but the presence of so many innocent bystanders was unprecedented in her experience.

I'm a slayer, not a cop! she thought. "All right, Danforth—Rick Church—or whoever you are. You have what you want. All four of you. You have Sarah and me right where you want us. Why don't you send these zombies back where they came from?"

"Oh, my dear, I am afraid we need them," said Danforth unctuously. "In order to guard all these hostages. And I am afraid we need these hostages as well, to keep you towing the straight and narrow."

"We cannot afford unpredictable events during the ceremony," said MacGovern/Mather.

"Thanks for telling her, you imbecile!" hissed Frank/Corwin.

"Excuse me. I am a judge," said Rick/Danforth.

"Excuse *you,*" said Buffy. "You're a man who doesn't know he's dead."

"What do *you* know about death?" snorted Lora/Heather.

"Been there, bought the T-shirt." Buffy gestured at the people. "Anyone of these people might do something you hadn't planned on and screw everything up until the next time the stars or whatever are right for you to try again. So you'll have to wait—what? Another three hundred years? Deal with the wait."

"She is right," said Rick/Danforth.

"I agree," said MacGovern/Mather.

"Kill them all," said Lora/Heather to the zombies.

Buffy tensed; the time had come to do or die. She just wished things had gone a little better before she died.

"No!" said Xander/Sarah. "You must wait!"

"Why is that?" sneered Frank/Corwin.

"I cannot speak for whoever has brought us here now," said Xander/Sarah, "but the Despised One would not have appreciated the fact that you arranged for his first feast, then slew everyone before he had the opportunity to make the first bite. I can imagine how the current Master gets when his appetites are not sated. You must not kill them. You must allow them to wait outside, unharmed."

"I get it," said Heather. "When the Master rises, he will know what to do with them."

Which is not *going to happen,* Buffy added to herself. Then: *The Master, eh? What a surprise. His decayed hand is all over this.*

The four looked at one another. Buffy kept one eye on the zombie army, another on the hostages and a third on the Freakin' Four. Were they silently communicating with each other?

Finally they turned to face Buffy and their captives. "I have made my decision," said Rick/Danforth.

"No!" said Lora/Heather. *"We* have come to our decision. Here we are all equals."

"I fear you have spent too long in the New World," said Rick/Danforth sadly. "It has affected your mind."

"Death has a way of doing that," said Buffy.

"In any case," said Frank/Corwin, "the end result is the same. Buffy—or should I say, Kane?— we will let these people leave the premises only on one condition: that you surrender yourself immediately." He held a rope out to a zombie, who lowered its assault weapon, took the rope and walked toward Buffy.

"Mind you, we did not say we would set the people free," said MacGovern/Mather. "The zombies will still guard them, and a few will remain behind to guard *us.*"

Reduction of odds. A good thing. Buffy decided. She was fairly positive no one noticed her bumping against a table as the zombie approached.

Other zombies, making weird growling noises that sent Billy Bob's customers down a spiral of terror, gestured with their weapons indicating the course the good citizens should take. Naturally the good citizens took it, some practically falling all over one another in their attempts to get out.

They all marched past Buffy while her hands

were being tied behind her back. Everyone, whether they be fearful, stoic, altruistic or among the injured, looked her in the eye. The zombies escorting them out did not encourage communication, but Edith was brave enough to muster a "Thanks, I won't forget this."

"You probably will," Buffy replied.

"Bet you a steak dinner I don't," said Edith.

"You're on," said Buffy.

"Silence!" said Rick/Danforth. "You, my young Slayer, are in no position to do anything."

"In fact," said Lora/Heather in conspiratorial tones, "we could ensure you won't be around to commit your treachery a second time by taking advantage of whatever instruments of torture the kitchen may provide."

"Slay them!" said Xander/Sarah desperately, turning to Buffy. "Why don't you slay them?"

"My hands are tied," replied Buffy. "And I try—whenever possible—not to kill my friends' bodies."

"You're not like Samantha Kane!" Sarah exclaimed.

"I'll take "Duh" for two hundred." said Buffy dryly.

"I think the Master would rather devour this Slayer personally," advised Frank/Corwin. "I believe they have a history."

"So do we," said MacGovern/Mather, "in our fashion. Come here."

That order was directed at Buffy, but she did not respond until the zombie behind her pushed her with its rifle. "Keep your head on. I'm moving," said Buffy testily.

"And just how would you slay us, young Slayer, in the unlikely event you ever have a chance?" inquired Rick/Danforth as he walked around his prisoner, inspecting her.

"I would drive a stake through your heart." She could not help glancing at Xander/Sarah who, though still cowering, had managed to slink to a chair.

"That wouldn't work on us," said Frank/Corwin with a laugh. "We're already dead."

"It would work on Eric Frank, though," pointed out MacGovern/Mather. "And that would seriously delay us."

Xander/Sarah nodded, as if she understood something. Buffy immediately got a bad feeling. While Buffy was reluctant to slay the living bodies of innocent people in order to thwart the heinous spirits of the dead, Sarah Dinsdale operated under no such personal restriction.

"Time for the ceremony," said Rick/Danforth.

"I think we need to fix the decor first," suggested Lora/Heather as she hefted a table over the bar.

"You got that right, woman! We need some ceremony room!" said Frank/Corwin as he kicked the table Sarah was sitting at with great gusto. The table smashed into other tables, sending them in different directions.

One of the remaining zombies happened to be in the way of a flying chair. The chair crashed into the zombie's putrid leg, which buckled and bent the wrong way, throwing the zombie off balance.

No one seemed to notice, not even the zombie.

"I need some more ceremony room!" Corwin shouted in delight. "Some ceremony room for the enlightened!" And he threw another table into the counter.

Xander/Sarah yelped as if bitten, then withdrew into herself as the three other possessed bodies commenced to tear up everything still standing in the steak house. Buffy couldn't blame her. This type of violence was so much more irrational than the kind found in the fight of good against evil.

The others threw themselves into the wanton destruction by ripping down those few things that had been left standing—jukebox, pinball machine, serving cart. And when everything was on the floor, the four of them worked together and threw everything up again. Maybe just to see how it fell into place.

"This is not enough ceremony room!" exclaimed Corwin in frustration.

Then they threw the stuff in the air again. Within a few moments Buffy realized there was some method to their madness. They were piling the debris with a definite pattern Buffy had seen before—in her dreams.

When she took into account the mess they were also making in the kitchen at the same time, she realized the piles were pale, smaller imitations of the stone slabs which had formed the boundaries the last time the ceremony had occurred.

"Hey, guys," said Buffy, "if the site in New England was a Pilgrim's Stonehenge, then is this a redneck Stonehenge?"

The possessed ones ignored her. Windows broke and the hokey sawdust that "flavored" the floor of Billy Bob's was stirred up. The rain began falling inside the steak house.

"Now is it time for the ceremony?" demanded Frank/Corwin.

"It is time," said Rick/Danforth. He walked into the kitchen. Or what was left of it.

The others followed, as did Xander/Sarah, meekly, and Buffy—but only because Frank/Corwin was pushing her.

They gathered around the grill. MacGovern/Mather carefully placed V.V. Vivaldi's Moonman sculpture on it, and the rock sizzled at once, filling the immediate vicinity with a terrible black smoke.

The four possessed ones chanted and danced. The moonrock glowed red-hot like a coal, only it remained whole; it did not, perhaps could not, burn. Even the heat generated by the grill was not enough to melt it.

"This is it," said Xander/Sarah. "He is coming! The Master is coming!"

Buffy thought she'd seen everything by now, but she'd never seen a mystical rupture in the space-time continuum before, where the boundaries between *here* and *there* vanished.

An altogether different kind of heat and smoke began to fill the room. The smoke curled out through the huge hole in the ceiling, while within a matter of moments the heat became suffocating.

"I'd forgotten what it was like to be human," said Rick/Danforth, trying to catch his breath.

"Quiet!" said Frank/Corwin. "The Master is coming!"

Indeed. A white hand whose skin combined the worst features of worms and reptiles rose up from the nothingness, followed by an arm wearing the sleeve of a dapper black jacket.

"How trendy," said Buffy. "Pale skin."

"Silence, insipid knave!" said Rick/Danforth.

"Have you no respect for your betters?" asked the Master. His head and torso had emerged. Both his hands were on the hot grill, no worse for the wear. He looked about wearing an expression of ecstasy. "I see you fixed the place up for me. How thoughtful."

"Would you care for a snack?" asked Rick/Danforth. "We thought you'd like to start with these two."

The Master looked at Buffy with a toothy grin. Buffy grinned back. *He* was the key to this whole nightmare.

At last the time to act had arrived. In the next few seconds she would know if she would live or die. *One thing is for certain,* she resolved. *Regardless of my fate, the Master will die. Again and again. Now I just need a distraction. . . .*

Buffy caught an unexpected movement from the corner of her eye. She turned to see Xander/Sarah holding an object while he/she rushed toward the Master with murderous intentions. "No!" Buffy exclaimed. "Use a *stake!* Not a *steak!*"

Sarah stopped in front of the grill and struck the Master several times on the chest and shoulders with the piece of meat.

The Master, halted in his emergence by this pesky human, took the steak from Sarah and held it gingerly between both fingers; he was clearly disgusted. "Do you realize how many nutrients were lost when they ruined this meat by cooking it?"

"Really? Looks a little rare to me!" said Buffy. Her hands were free—she had cut her bonds with the knife she had palmed earlier, when she'd bumped, seemingly accidentally, into a table. "Let's cut it."

She hurled the knife.

She was vaguely aware of Xander/Sarah showing a distinct lack of faith in her abilities by ducking, even though Buffy had planned on the knife missing him/her by a good half-inch.

Indeed. The knife spun right on course and thrust deep in the Master's chest.

"That's what I call a real steak knife!" said Buffy. "Game over."

The Master looked down in abject horror at the knife protruding from his body, but he couldn't bring himself to touch it. The sudden action broke the spell of the four chanters as they stopped in shock. The malevolent equilibrium dispersed and the gate between the *here* and the *there* began to disappear.

"You failed me!" he said to Rick/Danforth, the Master's voice rising in pitch. "I should have known. You're coming back with me! You're all coming back with me!" He held out his hand and closed it in a fist as if grabbing the four internal essences from thin air.

Then he fell back through the gateway.

The bodies of Rick and Lora Church, Darryl MacGovern, and Eric Frank fainted, collapsing into heaps.

"It's over," said Xander/Sarah. "Now I can leave this realm secure in the knowledge that I have made up for the evil I helped cause three hundred years ago."

"What about my friend Giles?" Buffy demanded. "Is he going to be okay?"

"His fever is already beginning to break, of that I am certain," said Sarah. "Farewell."

And Xander fainted, too, adding his body to the heap made by the other four on the floor.

The "living rerun" part of the night of the living rerun was over.

We now return to our regularly scheduled program.

"Thank goodness," said Buffy. "Now maybe I can get out of this stupid outfit."

CHAPTER 12

The rain ceased and the skies grew quiet. The wind still blew, but what came through the demolished steak house was warm and comfortable. After she had seen to it that everyone who hadn't started the evening as a corpse was still, Buffy rushed to the ladies' dressing room, which thankfully was still intact, pulled her clothes from the drier and changed. Then she returned to the kitchen and knelt beside Xander.

"Xander!" she hissed. When he didn't respond, she slapped him once.

His eyes opened immediately and he sat up. "Hey! That hurt!"

"Sorry, I had to make sure you were Xander. Are you okay?"

"Apart from a hot flash here and there, I think I'm fine."

"Phew!" exclaimed Darryl MacGovern, as he rolled into a sitting position. "Where did all these dead bodies come from? They sure do stink!"

"What happened?" asked Eric Frank with a groan. His hair looked like he'd stuck his finger in an electric socket.

"How did we did get here?" asked Rick Church.

"Oh my gosh! I look a fright!" exclaimed Lora Church, checking herself out in the reflection of a napkin dispenser.

Buffy guided Xander to what remained of one of the walls.

"What do you remember?"

"Everything," he said. "Up to a point. I still don't know what happened to Sarah Dinsdale after Kane put the kibosh on the Master. I'm afraid we both know what happened to Kane, though."

"But they don't seem to remember anything," said Buffy. "I guess when the Master yanked Mather and company from them, he took their memories too."

"The Master didn't want anything to do with Sarah," said Xander. "I know that. She went of her own accord. But where?"

"Phew!" said MacGovern behind them, as the wind shifted and a certain potent stench from outside wafted in like the aftermath of a stampede of skunks.

"What are they doing with those assault rifles?"

asked Eric Frank, pointing at pieces of zombies. He and MacGovern looked one another in the eye. "I smell a story here."

MacGovern, deep in thought, rubbed his chin. "You know, I think something paranormal happened here. I'd bet my reputation on it."

"You have no reputation," said Frank.

"Where's your crew?" asked Lora. "Shouldn't they be getting this on film?"

"Maybe they're in the van!" said Frank. "Let's find out!"

Let's go, mouthed Buffy to Xander, pulling him out the back door by his shirt sleeve. Then, once they were outside, "I think Eric Frank is going to have a difficult time explaining things to his crew."

"Really?" said Xander.

"Yeah, we'll probably read in the papers about how Billy Bob's was struck by a freak lightning storm," said Buffy.

"How will people explain all the dead . . . bodies?" Xander asked.

Buffy shrugged. "Mad corpse disease?"

Buffy and Xander found Giles and Willow sitting on the couch in his office.

"You made it, Buffy," said Giles, pleased, "but I hoped all along the Prince's prophecy was just an educated guess. I knew if anyone could untangle the complex web of fate, it would be you."

"Now you tell us," said Xander. "Oh, and thanks for being glad to see me."

"Well, I am," said Giles, not understanding the reason for Xander's sarcasm. "It's just that Willow and I were having a conversation about what you would call 'stuff.'"

"You mean 'things,'" said Buffy.

"Exactly. 'Stuff.'"

Xander waved his hand above his head.

"Ah," said Giles. "I'm talking over your head." He grinned. "A momentous occasion. If the two of you must know, I was telling Willow of the flashes I had of Robert Erwin's life before he died of that mystical fever. And we were wondering how much free will we really have—how free we are to make the choices that matter to us."

"You're always telling me I should forget about my private life and concentrate on my destiny and duty as Slayer," said Buffy.

"It's true that destiny has selected you," said Giles, "yet I would hope in the coming years you will find more freedom of choice than even you could have imagined possible."

"I'll remember that the next time I have a hot date," Buffy replied. "Or *any* date."

"Willow, you're awfully quiet," Xander observed.

Willow was surprised to have everyone's attention suddenly turn to her. "I was thinking. And wondering."

"About?" prompted Xander.

"Well, it's just that sometimes people choose their own destiny, you know, as in I've chosen to assist you two"—she pointed at Buffy and Giles—"in saving the world from various despicable creatures. But you two believe that destiny has more or less selected you."

"Yes," said Giles, nodding gravely.

"So what's your point?" asked Xander.

"How do you really tell? What if you two have made some massive mistake and you're not really the chosen Watcher and Slayer, and that I haven't been fated to make the same mistake with you?"

"I think you're reading too much into current events," Buffy advised.

Willow pouted. "Maybe. I've felt like such a fifth wheel this whole time."

The others immediately tried to buoy her confidence, pointing out how invaluable her assistance had been so many times in the past. If that wasn't destiny, Xander asked, then what else could it be?

"Better a fifth wheel than someone walking around in your skin. Yeesh!" Xander shivered. "I'm glad she's gone. Is my hair all right?"

After everyone had said good night and Willow walked home, her spirits plummeted again. This whole adventure confused her. It indicated bonds between the souls involved, but no love. To make matters worse, her soul, apparently, was not involved. And if there was anything Willow desired in this world, it was a bond between her and Xander even deeper, stronger than the one they now shared.

That, however, was not in the cards. Willow arrived home seriously bummed, a solitary person apparently for all time.

After staying up to watch a movie on the Romance Channel, Willow fell asleep with tears in her eyes. To say she felt lonely and depressed would be like saying the night is dark, or outer space is big, or there are too many reruns on TV in the summer.

Even so, her sleep was deep, and it wasn't long before she dreamed.

She dreamed of running through a heavily wooded forest—thicker, more teeming with life than any she'd ever seen—during a frightening thunderstorm of a strength almost as great as the storm that had struck Sunnydale while she'd been awake.

In this dream Willow felt older, heavier and distressed. She experienced a heartsickness so intense it was almost crippling. And yet some dread she could barely fathom propelled her through the woods, through the storm, toward a mysterious distant light that arced over the trees like a dome.

Whenever she noticed her clothing, though, she got the funny feeling she was no longer a she. For she wore a man's boots and a man's pants. The sleeves of the man's white cotton shirt were bloodied and tattered. Her breathing was labored, her every muscle ached, and her heart pounded at top speed.

A silent explosion, so odd its origin was surely evil, knocked Willow *the man* to the ground. When he got up the storm had diminished and the distant glow was fading. By now the glow wasn't so distant—only a few hundred yards away—but the man was stricken with spiritual agony. He had a hunger that would never be satisfied, a thirst that would never be quenched. He felt as if his life was over, though he was still young and strong.

Then he saw Sarah Dinsdale—also dirty and disheveled—running through the wood. He called out for her to wait, but she paid him no heed. He ran after her. He did not catch up to her until they had left the wood and were running down the beach, and even when he was able to touch her she did not stop.

So he tackled her. He landed on top of her and they struggled until he had both her hands in his grip and she was unable to fight back.

"Go on! Finish it!" she exclaimed. "Do what the others could not do and kill me! Isn't that what you always wanted?"

The man was so shocked he released her hands. "Absolutely not. Forgive me, but that was the last thing on my mind."

Something in his expression must have changed Sarah's mind about him, because she ceased to struggle and did not try to escape even though he was giving her plenty of opportunity.

"But you denounced me!" she said. "You denounced me before all of Salem."

The man stood, bowed his head in shame and

turned away from her. "It is true. I denounced you because I hated you. Rather, I thought I hated you. I did not know my own mind."

"A common enough affliction among men," said Sarah, "but presumably you know your mind today."

"Indeed I do. As I know my heart." He turned back toward her and she read something in his eyes that changed her expression to one of awe, and of a fear more tender and vulnerable than any he had ever before witnessed. "I love you, Sarah Dinsdale. I ask for more than your forgiveness. I ask for your heart. I ask for you to be my life partner."

"I wish I could believe you, but I am a witch. That I admit freely."

"Granted, but I have learned that not all witches are evil, just as all preachers, I am loathe to admit, are not as good as they might imagine."

She smiled and touched his cheek with her warm fingers. "Do not be dismayed to learn there is a bit of the devil in you. There is a bit of the devil in us all."

"I love you, Sarah. Come away with me. Let us leave this colony and go to Philadelphia. There we can change our names and no one will know of how you were wronged in Salem and of how I was the man who wronged you."

"You say that, knowing I cast a spell on you to make you love me?"

The man shrugged. "It made no difference. I

would have come to love you in time, spell or no spell. So what is your answer? Will you come away with me? Will you marry me?"

"When you put it that way, how could I say anything but yes, John Goodman?"

And Sarah/Xander kissed John/Willow. The two souls had made their connection, and forged their future together.

Willow Rosenberg smiled. She would sleep soundly tonight.

ABOUT THE AUTHOR

Arthur Byron Cover was born in the Dark Ages, a few years before the invention of rock and roll. He is currently old enough to remember a time before *Star Trek* and *Star Wars,* if there is such a thing. He repairs his wheelchair himself.

As an intellect, he was profoundly influenced by the Silver Age of Comics and the Edgar Rice Burroughs "paperback boom" of the early sixties. For a week or two he thought the Dave Clark Five was a better band than the Beatles because they had a guy who played saxophone and the Beatles didn't. After graduating from high school, he attended V.P.I., where he was a tepid antiwar protester one weekend. The rest of the time he spent reading science fiction. After graduation, he became profoundly influenced by Russian literature and more comic books. Not to mention classical music, progressive rock and electronic music.

Today Cover can safely say he's written several novels, a few of which sprang entirely from his own forehead, a handful of comic books, a couple of animation shows, various book reviews, and many drafts of two movie scripts. He has taught writing classes and has been co-host for a radio talk show dealing with science fiction and its sister genres. He manages a SF bookstore in Sherman Oaks, CA, and shoots the breeze a lot.

"YOU HAVE NO IDEA WHAT IT'S LIKE TO HAVE
DONE THE THINGS I'VE DONE . . . AND TO CARE."
—ANGEL

THE ANGEL CHRONICLES
VOLUME I

A NOVELIZATION BY NANCY HOLDER
BASED ON VARIOUS TELEPLAYS FROM THE HIT
TV SERIES CREATED BY JOSS WHEDON

Available mid-June

From Archway Paperbacks
Published by Pocket Books

1461

"Well, we could grind our enemies into powder with a sledgehammer, but gosh, we did that last night."   - Xander

BUFFY

THE VAMPIRE

SLAYER™

As long as there have been vampires, there has been the Slayer. One girl in all the world, to find them where they gather and to stop the spread of their evil and the swell of their numbers.

#1 THE HARVEST
A Novelization by Richie Tankersley Cusick
Based on the teleplays by Joss Whedon

#2 HALLOWEEN RAIN
By Christopher Golden and Nancy Holder

#3 COYOTE MOON
By John Vornholt

#4 NIGHT OF THE LIVING RERUN

By Arthur Byron Cover

All new adventures
based on the hit TV series created by Joss Whedon

 From Archway Paperbacks
Published by Pocket Books   1399-03

RICHIE TANKERSLEY
C U S I C K